Chaos at Camp

Amy Barkman

First Edition. Published by Voice of Joy Publications.
www.voiceofjoyministries.com

ISBN-13: 978-0-9983520-7-7
ISBN-10: 0-9983520-7-1

Printed in the United States of America.

Contents

Chapter One

Ready for Camp

"Maggie?"

One of the twins called from the hall. Her baby sisters shared the bedroom next to hers and often came to her room to ask for help with their hair or a craft project, or just to visit.

"Come on in," she called back. The door opened and she turned from where she'd been staring blankly at the computer screen.

Both Cindy and Celie came through from the hallway. As usual, the five-year olds were dressed alike, this time in matching ballerina costumes.

Maggie never got tired of looking at her sisters. They were so pretty. Where her brown hair was straight as a ruler, the twins' curls bounced all over their heads and made the sparkle in their eyes seem like it flowed all over, affecting every part of their body. She wondered if their ever-present joy had to do with being twins and never feeling alone.

Cindy was always the spokesperson for the two. "Can you look on the internet for us and see where we can write to Santa

Claus?"

"Sure, but why?" asked Maggie. "Christmas won't be for months now."

"We want to thank him," said Cindy. "We just thought of it. We thank everybody else but we don't ever thank Santa Claus."

Celie was nodding and Maggie suspected that the thank you had been her idea. She pulled up the search address and when it appeared, she typed in "Santa Claus address".

"Santa Claus, North Pole."

"That's all?" asked Cindy.

"That's it. No zip code or anything. I guess the post office gets so many for him that he doesn't have to have a special zip code."

"Thank you, Maggie," Celie's soft, seldom heard, voice touched her older sister's heart as usual. Celie always seemed so fragile and, indeed, she was the weaker of the two, always getting a virus or other sickness before her stronger twin and keeping it longer. Maggie hugged her sisters and the girls left, whispering together.

Maggie turned back to the computer. She'd been neglecting the e-mail pal that she was assigned at school. A girl from Texas named Kayla also signed up at her school for an e-mail pal. She and Maggie were paired together because they were the same age. At first Maggie thought they would have the same interests. But Maggie was bored with Kayla … they'd been writing to each other since last September and all Kayla wanted to talk about was boys. When Maggie told her about the Fun To Be One Camp that she and her friends were going to this summer, her pen pal didn't even write back about it.

With a sigh, Maggie downloaded her e-mail. There were some jokes from friends and a message from Kayla.

This message was different.

"Dear Maggie, I am really sad and I can't talk to my friends here. Can I talk to you? I know you won't tell anybody because you don't know anybody who knows me! LOL! Not really. I mean I'm not really laughing out loud. And I'm not laughing inside either. I just found out last night that my parents are getting a divorce. They don't know that I know it. I woke up in the night to go to the bathroom – I drank a coke right before bed, now I know why they say not to do that. I heard them talking so I stood outside their bedroom door and listened. They are planning on telling me as soon as school is out. I don't know what to do. Can you think of anything? Your sad friend, Kayla"

Maggie sat very still for a moment. Then she said out loud. "Okay, Lord. I can't think of anything at all. But you know everything. Will you tell me what to write to Kayla?" She waited but nothing came to her.

She waited longer. Still nothing came to her. "Jesus, Kayla needs your help. Please tell me something to say."

Nothing.

She almost turned off the computer but realized that she was the only person Kayla could talk to about her parents, so she couldn't just ignore the message. Finally she wrote:

"Dear Kayla, I am sad with you. I can't think of anything right now but I have prayed about it and I believe that one of us will hear something from God. I know that God doesn't want people to get divorced. And I know he loves you very much. When I'm sad, I pretend my pillow is Jesus' shoulder and I am curled up in his lap. Maybe you could do that until He tells you what else to do. I am asking him to make your parents' marriage better. And I am asking him to help you. Your friend, Maggie"

She hit the send button and then turned off the computer. After a minute she turned it back on and went to a search engine. Twenty minutes later she had requested prayer for Kayla's parents from ten different ministry prayer teams. Feeling better, she started to e-mail Kayla but remembered about Kayla trusting her to not tell anyone. She didn't think that requesting prayer for just "Kayla's parents' marriage" was a betrayal of trust, especially since she didn't know the last name and didn't even give the state. But Kayla might not see it that way. She better not say anything more until she heard from her friend again.

Before she got up, she prayed again.

"Thank you, Jesus, for giving me something to do about this. Please help me help Kayla. I think she probably doesn't know you. Please let me introduce you to her. Amen."

There were only three more days of school and everybody acted like vacation had already begun. While Ms. Gray was talking and writing things on the board, most of the class were throwing paper wads and whispering - even Gretchen, Maggie's best girl friend and member of the Fun To Be One Club. Well, Gretchen wasn't throwing paper wads but she was whispering to Danny who sat in front of her, and making him laugh.

It was a relief that this school year was over. It was a rough one. There was the witchcraft that started in the classroom the first day of school and the bullying that went on until Leo Bailey got expelled, and parents finding out about their secret club. But everything turned out okay and Maggie could hardly wait 'til time to go to camp.

"Maggie!" Ms. Gray was looking at her, with hands on her hips.

"Yes, Ma'am?" Uh oh. Maggie had no idea what she'd done.

"You didn't answer my question. Didn't you hear me?"

Ouch. Now what? Might as well be honest. "No Ma'am, I

didn't. I wasn't paying attention. I'm sorry."

"I asked you what your plans are for the summer."

Maggie smiled at her. "That's why I wasn't paying attention. I was thinking about going to camp."

"Camp? Girl Scout Camp?"

"No Ma'am. It's a camp for both boys and girls. It's called The Fun To Be One Club Camp." It felt strange to mention The Fun To Be One Club out in public. She and some of her friends had started a secret club and called it that before they found out there was a national one. But they still weren't going to tell anybody, except their parents, about their own private club.

Ms. Gray frowned. "What kind of club is that?"

"Um..." Maggie looked over at Gretchen who had stopped whispering to Danny. "It's, well, they have lots of fun stuff."

Danny raised his hand.

"Yes, Danny?" Ms. Gray switched her attention to him and Maggie relaxed.

"It's like a church camp. Only people from lots of different kinds of churches go there."

Maggie thought Ms. Gray kind of turned up her nose but she didn't say anything. She just turned back toward her desk. Maggie rolled her eyes and mouthed, "Thank you" to Danny.

He nodded. Gretchen smiled at her and shrugged.

After school the kids met at the Clubhouse which was an old chicken coop made over. Maggie was one of the first Fun To Be One Club kids, at least in their town. She, David, Ray, and Gretchen in her class, Polly who was a grade ahead of them, Kyleigh and Scooter, who were a grade behind, were the ones to form the Club last summer. During the school year, first Danny and, recently Harold, joined them.

Maggie looked at everyone getting their pillows out of the plastic bags. "Hey, I just noticed, we need to get some more girls in the Club. We've got more boys than girls now."

Ray grinned. "Well, until Danny came, we had more girls than boys! Now I think we need some more African Americans!"

Gretchen jabbed him with her elbow. "No, we need more Asians."

Polly laughed. "I refuse to say that we need more Native Americans."

Scooter frowned. "I think you just did." And they all laughed.

"Okay, you guys. I'll shut up about more girls." Maggie grinned at her friends.

Everybody grinned back except Kyleigh.

"What's wrong?" Maggie asked her.

"Nothing really, but I do wish there was at least one more Catholic."

Polly walked over to the younger girl and hugged her. "You know it doesn't matter what church we go to. That's the whole point. Fun to Be One - no matter what denomination we belong to."

Kyleigh nodded. "I know but at least you are all lumped together and called Protestants. I'm Catholic."

Maggie spoke quickly before anybody else could. "But that's what makes it fun - fun for God, anyway. We all know we belong to him whether we're Protestant or Catholic. Right?"

The younger girl wiped a tear away from her eye and smiled at Maggie. "Right."

"And you might meet some other Catholics at camp this summer."

When Maggie got home there was a note from her Mom on the front door. "Gone to the Doctor with twins. Cookies on table. Should be back by 5:30."

Maggie took three cookies, poured herself a glass of milk and headed upstairs. She turned on the computer and downloaded her e-mail. There was one from Kayla that had "good news" in the subject line. Great! God must have done something to make her parents want to stay together.

Maggie opened the message.

"Oh, No!" The words flew out of her mouth before she knew they were coming. Some moist crumbles of chocolate chip cookie flew out along with the words.

The message said, "Yay! I'm going to get to come to the Fun To Be One Club camp too. I think my parents would give me anything I asked for right now. We'll get to meet each other and spend two whole weeks together. Isn't that awesome?"

Chapter Two

Or Maybe Not!

"Mom! This is the worst." Maggie ran down the steps when she heard the car pull in the driveway. She burst out with her news as soon as Mom and the twins came through the front door. "That girl Kayla, my pen pal, is going to camp too. And she thinks I'm going to spend all my time with her. I don't want her to be there!" She could hear the whine in her own voice but she didn't care.

Mom hugged her. "I'm sorry, Sweetheart. How did she know about the camp?"

"I told her. I sure wish I hadn't."

The twins walked on up the stairs while Maggie followed Mom into the kitchen.

"Why were you at the doctor's office? Is something wrong?"

Mom was looking in the refrigerator and finally came out with a stick of butter. "No, just some tests." She went to the pantry and came out with a box of cornmeal mix. "I thought I might fix broccoli cornbread tonight. Would you like that?"

"Yum. It's my favorite. What else are we having?"

"Cube steaks and asparagus."

"Yes!" She started to leave the kitchen but had a funny feeling. "Mom, are you sure there's nothing wrong?"

Mom didn't say anything for a few seconds and then answered in a serious voice. "I don't know, honey. The doctor is doing some blood work on Celie. He wants to make sure there isn't anything wrong. You know, 'cause she's been sick so much this year."

"Like what could be wrong?" Maggie could feel her heart pounding in her chest all of a sudden.

"I'm not sure. Let's not borrow trouble. We'll see what the blood tests show."

"When will we know?"

"We should know by Friday."

Today was Wednesday.

"Danny, can I talk to you?" Maggie caught up with her other best friend as he was walking out the front door of the school Thursday afternoon.

"Sure," he smiled at her and moved over a little to make room for her to walk beside him on the sidewalk.

Maggie sighed. "I did a really stupid thing."

Danny looked at her curiously.

"I told my e-mail pen pal about the Fun To Be One Club camp. And now she's coming too."

"You don't want her to come?"

"No!" Maggie sighed. "I don't like her. She just talks about boys all the time. Well until lately ... " She remembered Kayla was trusting her not to tell anybody about her parents. And now that she was coming to camp, Maggie's friends would know her.

"What's she been talking about lately?" Danny asked.

"Oh, coming to camp and stuff like that."

Danny looked at her kind of funny but he didn't say anything.

Maggie sighed. "She expects to spend all her time with me and I want to spend all my time with you guys."

Danny grinned at her. "Maybe Kayla is 'one of us' and Jesus wants her to come to the camp."

Maggie remembered her prayer for Jesus to show her how to help Kayla. She groaned.

"What?"

"Kayla is not one of us. But I did ask Jesus to show me how I could help her. I guess He's showing me. But I don't want her to take away all my fun at camp."

"We won't let her, Maggie. We'll make sure you have some fun."

"Thanks, Danny. I appreciate it." They reached the place where they split to go to their different homes and said goodbye.

Uh-oh. Why was Dad's car in the driveway at this time of day? Maggie ran the rest of the distance between her and the front door. She burst in and could hear the twins giggling upstairs. She dropped her book bag on the couch and ran into the kitchen.

Mom was sitting at the kitchen table with tears streaming down her cheeks, and Dad was standing with his arm around her as she leaned against him.

"What's wrong?" Maggie asked the question but deep down she already knew the answer. "It's Celie, isn't it?"

Mom nodded and started sobbing. Dad held out his other arm and Maggie ran in to his embrace.

She waited for them to speak the word.

"Well, it looks like it could be … Leukemia," Dad said.

Maggie stamped her foot. "I hate it. I hate it!"

"We do too, Sweetheart." Dad pulled her closer to his chest. "But we're going to beat this thing. We caught it soon."

"B...but," Mom sobbed. "She'll have to have that bone marrow test and..." She couldn't finish the sentence.

"What?" Maggie pulled back out of the family embrace. She could feel the fury in her chest and on her face. "What's a bone marrow test? And what else will she have to do?"

Dad sat and pulled Maggie down in the chair next to him.

"The blood test showed an extremely high white cell count which is pretty definite proof of leukemia, but she has to go back and have a bone marrow test to make sure. That's where they stick a hollow needle into, probably her hip bone, and draw out some cells. That will show more definitely what the problem is."

"Ouch." Maggie glared at him. "And? Mom said 'Bone marrow test and...'"

Dad was his usual calm and kind self. "And if she definitely has it, she will have to have chemotherapy."

"No!" Maggie stood up. "That's where they get sick and lose their hair and get all skinny and stuff, right?"

Dad nodded. Mom had quit crying and looked at Maggie.

"Sweetie, we just need to pray hard that there was a mistake."

"You don't think so or you wouldn't be crying like that." Maggie glared at her Mom. "I'm not a baby."

"You're right," Dad answered. "We wouldn't have had the blood test done if we hadn't suspected this from her tiredness and lowered immune system. What we need to pray for is a miracle."

Maggie nodded. She always like to have a clear assignment. She started out of the kitchen but Dad called her back.

"You can't tell anyone. You know how gossip spreads. And we don't want Celie to hear about it. Not until we know for sure and tell her ourselves."

Maggie nodded and turned to go. Then she thought how selfish she was being. She ran to Mom and hugged her. "I'm sorry Mom. I'm going to pray for that miracle really hard."

Mom hugged her back and said, "Thank you, Sweetie. I will too."

Maggie let herself into the Fun To Be One Clubhouse. It was nice to be here by herself, in the place where she'd felt God's presence so many times. She was glad her parents said she could come. They understood. She really didn't think she could face the twins right now. They would know something was wrong.

She unwrapped her pillow, sat down on the floor, and closed her eyes. "King Jesus, I need you." She sat there for a long time, but she still felt all alone. Finally she got up and went to the ledge where the books were kept. She pulled out "Kingdom Tales" from the Fun To Be One Club library.

Her favorite story in the book was "Harmony, Rhythm, and the Wonderful Tree" so she opened to it. She read it more carefully and thoughtfully than she ever had. When she came to the end, she replaced the book back in the plastic bag.

"Okay, Jesus. In that story people got healed from the leaves of the wonderful tree. I want to know how that can help Celie. I want a wonderful tree here, now, in this place. Please tell me how to find one."

She waited to see if she could hear from Him. She'd felt his presence many times but today there was nothing. What was wrong with her lately? It seemed like every time she asked for help to help somebody else, all she got was silence. She bit her lip. She knew she shouldn't be mad at God, especially not at

Jesus who died on the cross for her. And for Celie.

"Don't you care, Jesus? Don't you care that Celie is going to have to go through all that awful stuff?" She realized she was yelling. At Jesus. That sure wasn't very Christian of her.

The door opened and David stuck his head through the door. "Maggie?"

David was the one who thought up their Fun To Be One Club in the first place. And he was the one who found out about the national Fun To Be Club and Camp. Of all the people to hear her yelling at Jesus! Maggie could feel her face turning red.

"Yeah, it's me." She crossed her arms and waited for the lecture.

But David just pulled out his cushion and sat down beside her. "What's wrong? I just got home and started playing a computer game and the King said to come here to the Clubhouse - and do it Now!"

At that, the tears that Maggie had been pushing down, came out in a gush. She sobbed and realized she sounded like her mother had earlier. David just sat quietly waiting.

Finally she stopped crying enough to talk. "Mom and Dad said I couldn't tell anybody. But you won't tell, will you?" She didn't even have to ask because she knew David was very trustworthy.

"Of course I won't tell. I'll just pray."

"They think one of my twin sisters has leukemia. They're pretty sure and she has to have a needle stuck into her hip and draw out bone cells or something and then if it is, she'll have to have chemotherapy and get skinny and go bald." At those last words, the tears came back. "I kn...know it's silly but she has th...the prettiest hair in the world."

David's voice was calm. "But it will grow back and you don't want her to lose her life."

Maggie hadn't even thought about that. Celie dead? She looked at her friend in horror, tears having fled in the cold shock of the possibility of Celie's death.

"NO!"

"Let's pray, Maggie. That's why Jesus sent me. So we could agree together in prayer."

Maggie nodded and gave him her hand.

"Father, thank you for sending me here today so Maggie wouldn't be alone in this bad time. You said whenever two of us are together in Jesus' name and in agreement, He is here and will do whatever we ask. So we're here and we agree that we want Celie to live and not have to go through all that chemotherapy and stuff. You can heal her and we're asking you to do it. And we believe you will, because you want her healed even more than we do. In Jesus' name. Amen." He turned to Maggie and smiled as he let loose of her hand. "There, it's done. Celie is going to be fine."

Maggie smiled back.

But she didn't believe it.

Chapter Three

To Go or Not To Go

Maggie had never felt so guilty in her life. The Bible said that whenever two are in agreement, Jesus was there and would do whatever they asked. But she wasn't really in agreement with David. She didn't trust that Jesus would heal Celie. Did that mean that Celie couldn't get healed, and all because her big sister didn't trust Jesus to do it?

As soon as she opened the door at home, after her time at the Clubhouse, the twins came and surrounded her with hugs and kisses.

"Where have you been? Why are you late coming in from school?" Cindy asked the questions.

Maggie grinned at them both. "Nosy Rosies! I was here earlier but went back out. And met a friend." That was true. She'd met David, even though she didn't plan it.

"We miss you when you're not here," Celie added in her shy whispery voice.

Maggie's heart felt like it turned over in her chest. How could she go off to camp and leave her baby sister at a time when she was facing the awful things that were going to happen to her? She didn't say anything but hugged them both.

After the twins were in bed, she went to her parents where they sat in the family room.

"When does this bone thing happen?"

"We won't know 'til the Doctor's office calls back and tells us when they can get an appointment." Mom patted the couch beside her and Maggie joined her.

Maggie looked over at her Dad, sitting in the chair across from them. "I don't think I should go to camp. Not while Celie is sick."

Dad's smiled at her with a sadness in his eyes. "Sweetheart, I think it would be good for you to get away during this time."

Maggie swallowed hard against the lump in her throat. "But Celie said ... " She wiped a stray tear from her cheek and bit her lip. "She said she missed me when I'm gone. So I can't desert her now!"

Mom put her arm around Maggie's shoulder. "It's two weeks from this coming Sunday before the Camp starts, so let's just wait and see what happens."

Dad nodded. "When you're really upset about something, especially when you just find out about it, it's not good to make decisions right away." He smiled and winked at Maggie. "Okay?"

She nodded. And took a deep breath. She wanted to tell them about David's prayer and ask if her fears would keep it from working. But they'd told her not to tell anybody. So she just turned to hug Mom and got up and hugged Dad on her way out of the living room and up the steps to her bedroom.

Friday, the last day of school before summer break. At

lunch the Clubhouse kids sat together as usual. Danny opened the conversation but he didn't want to talk about camp or their own club.

"Just think, two weeks from tomorrow Coach will be my stepdad." Danny grinned from ear to ear and Maggie couldn't help grinning with him. Last year had been a major change in Danny's life. He and his Mom moved from the city and his Mom worked in the lunchroom here at school. She and everybody's favorite teacher, Coach Adams, got to know each other and were getting married this summer, the day before the club kids left for camp.

Most of the Fun To Be One Club kids were going to be in the wedding. Maggie thought that was yuck but she was going to do it, for Danny.

"And then Fun To Be One Club Camp. And then I go spend a month in Texas with my biological Dad!" That was another thing that happened for Danny this year. He hadn't seen his father since he was three years old and didn't ever want to see him again. But Mr. Alcorn had changed and was a really nice man now. And Danny had a younger brother he'd never known about.

David answered first. "We're all glad for you, Danny."

Gretchen, Ray, and Harold all nodded.

Maggie said, "We really are, Danny." And she really was. She'd liked Danny from the first time she met him. She'd even fought the others to include him in their Club. And she was right! Danny was one of those who could hear the King's voice well. A lot better than she could, that was for sure!

As they were taking their trays up to stack them to be washed, Maggie whispered to David, "Can you come to the Clubhouse after school? Just for a few minutes?" They'd all met officially for the last time of the school year on Wednesday because some of them had family things to do right after school today. She hoped David wasn't one of them because he was the only one she could talk to without disobeying Mom and Dad. Well, she'd disobeyed already but David said Jesus sent him to talk to her, so that made it okay. She hoped.

David nodded.

David was already there when Maggie got to the Clubhouse. Gretchen and some of the other girls in her class took a long time in saying good-bye; most of them wouldn't see each other until school started again.

"What's up?" David asked as soon as she walked through the door.

"I want you to pray about something. I need to know if I should go to the Fun To Be One Club Camp or stay home with Celie."

"But Celie is going to be fine, so why wouldn't you go?" David looked at her with a question in his eyes.

Maggie pulled out her pillow and sat on it. She finally looked in David's face. "I have a confession. I'm having a lot of trouble believing that. I mean believing that Jesus will heal Celie. And I feel really bad. Will my doubting keep Celie from getting healed?"

David had obviously been planning on staying just a minute or two but now he pulled his own pillow out of the plastic cover and sat down facing Maggie. He didn't say anything to her but bowed his head.

"Okay Lord, I don't know the answer to Maggie's question. But you do. I want you to give Maggie faith to believe you to heal Celie. And I want you to tell her whether to go to camp or not. In Jesus Name, Amen."

Then he sat in silence like they always did after a question prayer, waiting for the answer.

It surprised Maggie when words came to her mind really

strong, almost like they were spoken out loud. "Go to camp."

Her eyes flew open and she saw David still with his head bowed. She closed her eyes again and said out loud. "Okay, I'll go to camp. But can you tell me if I'm keeping you from healing Celie?"

Nothing. She waited. Opened her eyes again and saw that David hadn't moved. Closed her eyes again. Waited. Nothing. She sighed.

"Okay, David. I guess all the King is going to tell me is to go to camp."

David opened his eyes and kind of squinted them. "I think the two answers are all mixed in together." He shook his head. "I think when you go to camp, you'll find out some things." He shrugged his shoulders. "Or something like that."

Maggie nodded. "Okay." She got up and began putting her pillow back in the wrapping. "Thank you for coming. I know I was able to hear Him because you were here praying."

"You're welcome. And I'm praying for your sister." He grinned. "And I believe she's going to get healed!"

Maggie grinned back. "Thank you."

Danny's mother and Coach Adams were going to have a small wedding on Saturday afternoon at the Methodist Church. The groomsmen were going to be Danny and David and Ray. And the bridesmaids were going to be Maggie and Gretchen and Polly. Maggie tried to be excited about dressing up in the long pink gown that matched her friends' but it was hard to be excited about anything when all she could think of was her baby sister having to have needles stuck in her hip.

It seemed to take forever for the Doctor to call back with a date for that awful test. And when he did tell them, it was going to be on the Monday of Maggie's second week at camp. Maggie would have argued to stay home if it hadn't been for those strong words, "Go to camp."

It was kind of neat that there wouldn't be anything yucky before the wedding. And it was really neat that her Mom and Danny's Mom were becoming friends.

When school had been out a week, Mrs. Alcorn and Gretchen and Polly and their Moms all came to Maggie's house to see how the girls' dresses and little flower tiaras and shoes all matched. Maggie thought the moms were more excited about it than she and her friends were.

Well, definitely more than she was. Who cared about all that sissy girly stuff?

But when she saw how Polly and Gretchen smiled as they looked at themselves in the mirror, she thought maybe it was just that she was weird. As usual!

Mom made tea and scones with cream cheese and jam and they all sat around the dining room table and talked, after the dresses and stuff got put up. One of the other ladies that worked in the school lunchroom was going to be Mrs. Alcorn's matron of honor. And Coach Adam's pastor was going to be his best man. That seemed weird but since their pastor at the Methodist church was performing the wedding, Maggie guessed that was how Coach made sure his own pastor was included.

Mrs. Alcorn was telling Mom and the other women how much she liked the pastor of the non-denominational church.

"I have to confess I was really judgmental at first about that church. Danny wanted to go there but I thought they were some kind of cult or something. I was wrong and now we've been with Jerry several times on Sunday night. And I like it!"

"Mom," Maggie interrupted the women. "Can I take Polly and Gretchen up to my room?"

"Sure. You girls go on."

Whew! Now they could be normal again.

Dad took the twins out before the company got there so that all the women could talk and the girls could try on clothes without anyone else around, so the upstairs was empty. Gretchen had been there before but it was Polly's first time to be at Maggie's house.

"This is a really nice room." Polly looked around nodding her head. Maggie knew she was lucky – no, blessed, as David reminded them all the time – to have such a big room all to herself. One wall was all bookshelves filled with all kinds of books from "The Poky Little Puppy" and "The Little Engine That Could," to "Heidi" and "Little Women," to "Black Beauty," the "Chronicles of Narnia "and "Pride and Prejudice." In between some of the books and in front of some others were statues of horses. Maggie loved horses and that was one thing she'd been looking forward to about going to the Fun To Be One Club camp. They offered horseback riding lessons.

Gretchen answered Polly. "Yes, I had to make myself not be jealous when I first came here. I have to share a room with my older sister."

Polly nodded. Her ancestry was American Indian. Maggie always wondered if Polly's habit of few words was because of her race or just her personality. Maggie didn't know any other native Americans.

She wished Gretchen hadn't said anything about sisters. The lump in Maggie's throat that had been threatening to choke her for the past week came back. And when she tried to swallow it, tears squeezed out of her eyes. Polly was the first to notice.

"Maggie, what's wrong?"

The words just seemed to spill out of her mouth. "I don't want to go to camp."

But she couldn't tell them why.

Chapter Four

We're Off to See...

The wedding was beautiful. Maggie had to admit that, even though she felt a little silly dressed up in front of the people there in the church. Polly and Gretchen loved it. Gretchen said it made her feel like a princess.

Danny and the other boys were in tuxedos. That made Maggie want to giggle but she controlled herself. What she really loved were the flowers. Pink and white roses were everywhere, at the end of the pews, in front of the altar, and in their corsages and the boys' ...

She'd said something really stupid when she saw the guys out in the hallway headed one way while they were headed the other way. The guys just had to walk in at the front of the church. They didn't have to parade down the aisle like the girls. She was just trying to be nice. She'd never seen guys wearing flowers before.

"I like your corsages!"

Ray started laughing and she could see Danny and David holding back smiles.

David said, in his gentle voice, "Boutonnieres, they're called boutonnieres."

The girls walked slowly up to the front. Coach and the boys were there facing them and watching them walk, which made Maggie feel even sillier. When they got to the front of the church, the girls then turned back toward the aisle and the organ started the wedding march. Everybody in the church stood up and a little girl from the kindergarten at school came in, dressed in a lighter pink than their dresses, scattering pink and white rose petals all along the aisle. Now Maggie understood why there was a plastic mat all down the aisle on top of the carpet; those roses would have smushed into the carpet and left stains.

Then Mrs. Alcorn came in. Wow! She was really pretty. She'd always been pretty but she looked like a real princess today. Her wedding dress was white at the top, and pink and white on the skirt which was spread out like the old time prom dresses Maggie saw in her Mom's old picture album. Mrs. Alcorn wasn't wearing a regular bridal veil over her face but she had on a crown with some net coming out in the sides and back. The net was both pink and white.

Maggie glanced over at Coach who was smiling all over his face. Danny was looking the same way. She guessed they both were proud of Mrs. Alcorn. Hmm. In a few minutes she would have a new name and be Mrs. Adams. Maggie hoped she would remember and call her the right name. Then she thought that would be good for Danny's mom if she had anything with initials on it. Her initials wouldn't change.

Mrs. Alcorn's father walked her down the aisle and when the pastor asked, he said that he and her mother gave her to Coach. Maggie could feel her lips tighten up. How dare parents give somebody away to somebody else, like they were a puppy or a goldfish or something?

Then came the mushy stuff.

Coach and Mrs. Adams made promises to love each other forever and that each of their families would belong to the other people's families, and a bunch of other stuff.

Then the preacher said some things about marriage but Maggie didn't hear much of it cause she noticed that Danny's nose was dripping. She guessed he must have a cold but how embarrassing to have your nose drip right there in front of the whole church.

Then it was over and Coach and Mrs. Adams, yay she remembered, walked down the aisle and out into the vestibule. Then the flower girl and Coach's pastor and the lady from the school lunch room followed them.

Then it was her turn. Danny held out his arm and she hooked hers around his like they taught her and joined the parade back down the aisle. She guessed Danny must have wiped his nose on his tuxedo sleeve at some time cause he looked okay again.

There was a party afterwards in the basement of the church. They called it a reception and there were nuts and punch and veggies and dip. Then there was the wedding cake. Maggie hoped they'd smash cake into each other's faces like she'd seen on You Tube, but they didn't. They just looked at each other all goo goo eyed, and politely put the bites of cake in each other's mouths. Boring!

Then it was finally time to blow bubbles at the bride and groom as they went to their car. They both stopped and hugged Danny and Mrs. Adams hugged her Mom and Dad. And then they were gone.

As they watched the car drive away, Maggie asked Danny, "What are you doing now?" She hadn't gotten to talk to Danny since school was out. Everybody had been so busy.

"Gramma and Grampa are spending the night with me.

They rented a car in Lexington when they flew in. And then they'll take me to David's tomorrow after church, before they go back to the airport."

She nodded. "I guess I'll see you at David's then." David's parents, Mr. and Mrs. Sanders, had a big van and were taking a group of them to the Fun To Be One Club Camp tomorrow afternoon. She and Polly were going with Ray, Danny, and David. Harold was going with Scooter's family along with Gretchen and Kyliegh.

But Maggie still didn't want to go.

The next day she hugged her Mom good-bye in front of David's house while her Dad put the suitcase and duffle bag into the van.

"You're going to have a wonderful time," Mom said and rubbed noses with her, the way she'd done when Maggie was little.

Maggie just looked at her through narrowed eyes. She was going for one reason and one only. The King had told her to.

She turned to the twins. Her heart hurt for both of them. They knew that Celie was going to have a test but they didn't understand. "Love you guys." She hugged them both to her side.

"We love you too, Maggie." Cindy smiled at her.

Celie just nodded and smiled without saying anything.

"I'll be praying for you guys while I'm gone, okay?"

The girls both looked puzzled. "Okay," said Cindy.

"We'll pray for you too, Maggie," whispered Celie.

When Dad had given her his goodbye hug, Maggie got in the van with her friends. The van pulled away and the last thing she saw as they turned the corner was her family all blowing kisses at her.

It was a three hour drive to the Fun To Be One Club Camp. They all sang songs and played 'I spy' during the ride. And they stopped after two hours to get gas and go to McDonalds for a snack. None of them had much lunch before they left.

Finally they pulled in to their destination. Maggie was surprised to see that the entrance didn't say Fun To Be One Club Camp. There were signs pointing to the camp off to the right. But other signs said that The Kingdom Project and King's Shoppes were straight ahead and the King's Chapel and Retreat Center were off to the left. And it seemed like way back, behind a forest of trees, straight ahead, she could see the top of a castle, with turrets and towers.

Maggie looked over at Danny and he just shrugged.

Polly said, "This is bigger than I thought."

Harold and David both said "Me too" at the same time.

David's Mom laughed. "You didn't look at anything online but the Fun To Be One Club, did you? We followed the other links and found out that the Club and Camp are part of a project that is huge. It's designed to bring Christians of all ages together."

Danny was the first to speak. "That's really cool."

Ray agreed. "That rocks!"

They turned to the right and pulled up in front of the main building, which looked familiar to Maggie because she'd seen it online so many times. It looked kind of like an English Tudor house and kind of like a Gingerbread House. She loved it.

Mr. Sanders parked the van in a small parking lot that said it was for registration only. And they all jumped out.

"Let's go check in," Mrs. Sanders said as she led the way into the Clubhouse.

When they walked in the door, Maggie couldn't stop herself from smiling. There beside the check-in desk was a knight in shining armor. Well, she guessed it was probably just empty shining armor without the knight. The ceilings were tall and there were chandeliers hanging down that looked like a lot of candles hooked together. The floors were wood, the kind with wide boards. Across from the desk were a bunch of really comfortable looking couches.

Maggie wanted to explore but Mrs. Sanders touched her shoulder and pointed to the desk.

"This is Maggie Kelly," she said to the lady standing there. The lady looked through some papers and pulled one out.

"Here you are," she smiled at Maggie. "We sure are happy you are coming to the Fun To Be One Club Camp. This is your first time?"

Maggie nodded. "Yes Ma'am."

"We are glad to have you. It's all paid and ready. You are in Cottage A, called Peace Cottage." She turned to Mrs. Sanders. "It's the first one on the right as you drive around the circle."

Maggie listened as the others checked in, disappointed when she heard the lady tell Polly she was in Cottage C, Joy Cottage. But maybe Gretchen would be in Peace Cottage too. She sure hoped so. Anybody but Kayla. *Please God, don't let Kayla be in my cottage.*

The boys were all in different cottages too. Maggie guessed that they always put everybody who knew each other in with different people. She hoped they knew that she and Kayla were pen pals so they would be in separate cottages.

Since Maggie's cottage was the closest, she was the first to be dropped off. Mr. Sanders took her suitcase and duffle bag to the door and knocked on it. When the door opened, he nodded to the one who answered, set the bags down, said to the girl there, "This is Maggie Kelly," and said to Maggie, "Have a wonderful time."

She watched him walk back to the van and waved at the

others.

Danny shouted out the window. "See you later!"

She was glad they'd been told that they all ate together at the Clubhouse. If she didn't know that, she would probably have done something stupid like cry. She saw the van pass one cottage and stop at the one after that. So none of them were far apart. That was a relief.

When she picked up her things and started in the door, the tall pretty girl who opened it was standing there smiling. "Hi, I'm Sarabeth. Welcome to Peace Cottage."

"Hi, I'm Maggie Kelly. Are you in this cottage too?"

Sarabeth smiled. "Yep. There's one of us older ones in every cottage."

She looked nice so Maggie laughed. "To make sure we act right?"

Sarabeth laughed too. "Well, I guess ... if you act bad. But mostly for if you need anything."

Maggie could feel her muscles relax. This wasn't going to be so bad. The cottage was nice, wood floors like the Clubhouse but more rustic. There was an open area that you walked into and a small kitchen at the back. Couches and a big table with twelve chairs filled the room. There were four doors leading from that room and she followed Sarabeth through one of them, the first door to the right. There was a bunk bed and a twin bed, a chest of drawers, a closet, and a sink with a big mirror above it.

"This is one of the four bedrooms in Peace Cottage. You can have your choice of beds since you're first. Twin top, twin bottom, or single."

"Can I have the single one?"

"Sure. Oh, I hear another car out front. Make yourself at home."

Sarabeth left the room and soon she could hear her saying

the same words she'd greeted her with. "Hi, I'm Sarabeth. Welcome to Peace Cottage."

Then she heard the response.

"I'm Kayla Burnett. Is there a girl named Maggie in this cottage?"

Chapter Five

O No, Not That!

"Yes," Sarabeth answered Kayla. "Are you talking about Maggie Kelly?"

"I don't know her last name. We are penpals through e-mail, from school. She's the one who told me about the camp."

Maggie stood there listening with her heart getting heavier and heavier. This was her worst nightmare about camp coming true. She clenched her teeth but then heard, deep inside, "You asked Me. Now here's your chance."

Maggie left her things still packed on the bed and stepped out of the door and into the main room. "Kayla? Is that you?"

The very overweight dark-haired girl's face lit up. "Maggie, they did put us in the same cottage! I'm so glad."

Maggie went over and hugged the girl. She'd never seen a picture of Kayla and had just thought, because she talked about boys all the time, that her pen pal was probably one of those really pretty girls with a good figure that some boys acted all silly about. Not her friends but some. She turned to Sarabeth.

"Will it matter that we know each other, I mean just by e-mail, not in person. Can we both stay in Peace Cottage?"

The tall blonde thought a moment and then said, "This is a different kind of situation. So, tell you what. I'll just keep quiet about the relationship but you have to be in separate rooms. Okay?"

"Okay."

The words they said in church every Sunday morning came to Maggie's mind: God is good, All the time. All the time, God is good.

Kayla looked sad but followed Sarabeth off to the room at the back on the left. Maggie breathed a deep sigh. They wouldn't even be sharing a bathroom.

But already she felt different about Kayla. She didn't seem like one of those snobby girls.

By the time Maggie had all her things unpacked, two other girls joined her and took the bunk bed. They seemed nice too.

Whitney was a pretty blonde and the other girl whose name Maggie forgot as soon as she said it, had red hair and freckles. She kind of reminded Maggie of Kyliegh who was Irish. Maybe Kyliegh really would find another Catholic friend there.

 Maggie's two roommates didn't know each other either so everybody was just starting out new. That made a difference. Nobody felt left out. Now Maggie understood the rule. If Gretchen and Polly, or even Kyliegh, who was younger, had been here, there would have been a bond between them that would have made the others feel left out whether they meant to or not.

The sound of a handbell being rung brought all the girls to the four doors to look out into the main room. Sarabeth stood there smiling. "If you've about finished unpacking, come on out and let's get to know each other before it's time to go to the Clubhouse. We have about forty five minutes before time to leave for supper."

All eleven girls joined their cottage leader at the table. Kayla made sure she sat beside Maggie.

Sarabeth handed out a folder to each of them and then sat in the chair at the head of the table. "Your folder has the schedule for this week. Some of you are just here for one week, some for two."

Maggie's heart leaped. Maybe she could go home after a week. And be there for Celie during the test that Monday.

"There are some blank sheets of paper, a sign-up sheet, and a pen for you to use too."

Sarabeth had them all tell their names and where they were from and what kind of church they went to. Sure enough, her other roommate was named Mary Katherine and she went to a Catholic church. Maggie couldn't wait to tell Kyliegh. Whitney went to a non-denominational church. Kayla said Methodist, but Maggie thought she just said that because she knew Maggie was a Methodist, and she figured Kayla didn't go to church anywhere. Of the other seven girls, two were Baptist, one was Presbyterian, one more was Methodist, one was Lutheran, and two were Assembly of God.

Sarabeth said she was also non-denominational like Whitney. Then she went over the rules. If anybody had a cell phone, they had to give it to her cause they agreed to not bring one when they signed up to come. And nobody could go to other cottages without her permission. And everybody had to fill out the paper in their folder that showed what kind of workshops, crafts and lessons they wanted.

Maggie knew her parents had already signed her up for horseback riding lessons but checked that anyway. She was trying to decide what kind of craft she wanted to learn when Sarabeth said, "Kayla, don't look on Maggie's paper. We want to know what you want to do, what you like."

She felt sorry for Kayla and turned to smile at her and

shrugged her shoulders. Kayla smiled back and shrugged her shoulders too.

Maggie chose drawing for a craft. Then she looked at the lessons.

Right there in front of her eyes, the third lesson down was "Biblical Healing." Yes! That's why God had her here. She would find out how to get Celie healed. That made it all worthwhile.

To Maggie's surprise, everyone was allowed to sit wherever they wanted for supper which was at the neat place where they checked in, the Clubhouse. As soon as her cottage group walked in, she heard cries of "Maggie, over here!"

Her friends from home were all seated together at a table. Each table only had eight chairs but they had squeezed another one in and pointed to it to let her know it was saved for her. She wanted to run and join them but there was Kayla. And there was also Love Himself in her heart saying again, "Now's your chance." She couldn't just run off and desert the girl.

"Come on," She motioned to Kayla to follow her to the table.

"Hey, guys. This is my pen pal. We're in the same cottage. Isn't that neat?" She purposefully didn't look at Danny. "Is there room for both of us?"

David jumped up and looked around for another empty chair. "Be right back," he said.

In a few minutes the ten of them were squeezed in around the table. Maggie hoped an adult wouldn't come and make them move.

"Hey, Kyliegh, guess what?"

The younger girl smiled. "What?"

"Mary uh, Mary somebody in my cottage is Catholic, just like you!"

"Mary Katherine," Kayla added.

Kyliegh grinned. "There is another Catholic girl in my cottage too! You all were right." She looked around the table and smiled at them. "And I got to be in the same cottage as Polly."

Maggie guessed there weren't enough cottages to separate them all. So they put the oldest and youngest together.

Danny said, "I'm hungry. When do we get to eat?"

Just then a man stood up at the front of the room where they could see buffet tables spread out behind him. He was older than Maggie expected the staff there to be, with a gray beard, and he wore some kind of a cap on his head, kind of like a beanie.

"Welcome to the Fun To Be One Club Camp dining hall. I'm Abe. I'll explain how this works and then you can get started. We have six cottages, three for guys and three for girls. This next two weeks we have you kids that just finished fifth, sixth, or seventh grade. Eleven kids in each cottage with one senior high school student who has been approved by the staff. After supper, we'll introduce you to some of the staff but for now, the Seniors will direct your table when to come up and fill your plates. You'll need to pick up napkins, forks, spoons, and knives too. Someone will come around to your table with drinks. And the desserts will be put out later." Then he led them in a blessing for the food.

The delicious smell had already told Maggie to prepare for fried chicken and sure enough, there it was. And lots of legs, her favorite. She noticed there were no wings or thighs, just legs and boneless breast pieces. Must be that kids liked those two best. There were also green beans and peas and macaroni and cheese. Maggie took two chicken legs and then wondered if that was okay. She looked around and saw Sarabeth leading a table up to get in line. Maggie got out of line and walked toward her.

"Sarabeth, is it okay to take two legs?"

The older girl nodded. And grinned. "Just make sure there's at least one left for me!"

Maggie felt embarrassed for Kayla when she came back with her plate piled so high with food that all the kids stared at it. No one said anything, though, and Maggie was glad. She noticed four chicken legs and two breast pieces piled on top of each other with macaroni and cheese squishing into them from two sides. No wonder Kayla was so fat.

And she talked with her mouth full. "So, tell me all your names."

David swallowed his food and said, "I'm David."

Polly and the others followed by telling their names too. Then they were all quiet. It was awkward, hard to be themselves with a stranger at the table.

But Kayla didn't seem to feel awkward at all. "The bunch of you really are politically correct, aren't you? Black, White, Indian, Asian. Why don't you have someone Hispanic in your club?"

With that Gretchen jerked forward with a cough and then clutched at her throat. Her eyes widened and it was obvious that fear was widening them. Before anyone could call for a staff member, Kayla jumped out of her chair and ran around behind Gretchen.

She bent over and said in a soft voice, "Can you breathe?"

Gretchen shook her head. Kayla bent over and did what Maggie knew was the Heimlich maneuver, put both hands at Gretchen's mid-section and pushed in and up. She did it three times and suddenly a piece of chicken skin flew out of her mouth and across the table to hit Ray in the mouth.

Maggie was torn between panic for Gretchen and a desire to laugh at the shock on everyone's face as they stared at Ray.

Then Gretchen took a deep breath and turned to Kayla.

"Thank you so much. You saved my life." She coughed and breathed deeply again.

"And you messed up my face," Ray grinned as he took a napkin and wiped the chicken off his mouth.

"I'm so sorry," Gretchen said.

"Just kidding," Ray answered. "Thanks Kayla. I was thinking 'Heimlich maneuver' but it seemed like I was frozen."

They all thanked Kayla, and Maggie relaxed. Maybe God had planned this whole thing with Kayla coming to camp. It wasn't going to be as awkward, since she'd made a place for herself in the group and wasn't just Maggie's tag-along.

At least Maggie hoped so.

Chapter Six

The Best and the Worst

The guy with the gray beard stood up front again ... Abe, she remembered his name.

"Now it's time to introduce you to the staff. And I want to thank the Directors for letting me greet you tonight. I don't get to come very much but I love the Kingdom Project and the Fun To Be One Club. Amy?"

A lady walked up to join him, followed by another man. They weren't young either. Why had Maggie thought everybody in charge would be the age of her parents?

"Thank you, Abe." The lady smiled out at them, and the twinkle in her eyes and something about her smile seemed, to Maggie, to hold some kind of secret. Like she had some surprises in store for them.

"I'm Amy and this is my husband, Gary. And you've already met our good friend Abe.

Can I see a show of hands of those who have been here before?"

About a third of the kids raised their hands.

"Okay, I hope I don't bore you with old information but we do have some exciting new things going on this year. A new study class and two new sports offerings to start with. " She motioned to several adults who were standing by the windows. Younger adults, the kind Maggie'd expected to see.

"This is Beth and Brian," she pointed to a smiling couple. "They will hold the 'Become All God Created You to Be' class for those who signed up for that." The two smiled and nodded toward all the tables. "Gary and I will be holding the 'Biblical Healing' class. Gary, do you want to say anything?" The man next to her just smiled and shook his head.

Maggie thought she'd rather have the younger couple as teachers but, oh well. Mostly she just wanted to learn how to get Celie well again.

"Sean and April will teach the 'Learning the Bible the Easy Way' class." Another couple stepped forward and smiled at them. "And Daphne and Chelsea, who are mother and daughter, will be teaching the 'Arts and Crafts' class. Next week, Chelsea will hold one of our new programs, the Archery Class." They too smiled out at the kids sitting at the tables.

Just then the double doors to the outside opened and a lady in jeans came in. She was a very small lady with long hair and Maggie wasn't sure how old she was.

"Ah! Patty! Kids, for those of you who signed up for horseback riding, this is your instructor, Patty. She's the best with horses and you're going to love working with her."

Patty grinned at everybody but stayed by the door.

Amy continued, "The water sports instructor isn't here yet. Water sports are the other new addition to the camp. You'll meet him tomorrow, those of you who signed up for any of those classes. I guess your seniors have already been through the schedule and you'll see that the study kind of classes will be in the mornings between breakfast and lunch, and the hands-on classes will be in the afternoons. That's to keep you from falling asleep after lunch during studies."

Everybody laughed. Well, it seemed like everybody in the room laughed - except Kayla. She had a hateful look on her face as she watched the Director speak. What was her problem?

"And," Amy went on speaking "Abe will be teaching the "Old and New Covenants" class, our new study class, which meets in the morning." She grinned at Abe before looking back at the tables. "Hope he doesn't send you to sleep *before* lunch!" Everybody laughed. "Seriously, this class is a very important one. Well, they all are. But healing and becoming all you can be both rely on the Covenants God made with man. And the "Learn the Bible the Easy Way" class will also be based on the covenants. Abe's class will just be a little more in-depth." She turned around to look at all the instructors. "Anybody want to add anything? Feel free!"

At first nobody moved, and then the lady named Beth raised her hand. "I just want to say that Brian and I are really excited about this class to help you who are taking it become all you can be. We expect it to be a life changer!"

Some applause broke out from one table and a boy shouted out, "It will be!!!"

Brian grinned and said, "Hi, Kyle!" Then he looked at the rest of them. "Kyle was in our class last year! How's that for good advertisement?"

Everybody laughed again.

"Okay, I'm going to say a prayer now and then we'll dismiss and you can go back to your cottages with your seniors. But there is an event planned for later tonight back here and they will tell you about it." Amy bowed her head. "Father, thank you so much for this new group of campers. They are at one of the most important times of their lives and I thank you so much for sending them here to have fun and prepare them for the future. Bless them, teach them, keep them safe, and fill them with joy! In Jesus' Name, Amen." She looked up and grinned, "See you later!"

Back at the cottage, they all had to listen as Kayla retold the story of Gretchen getting choked and how Ray knew what to do but froze. And how Kayla saved the day.

Maggie was partly embarrassed for Kayla and how she was bragging on herself, and partly irritated at her.

Sarabeth looked over at Maggie. "Why didn't anyone report this to the staff or at least one of the seniors?"

Maggie shrugged. "It was all over so fast and Gretchen was okay. I don't think any of us thought we needed to."

The Senior just nodded. Maggie wondered if she really thought it ought to be reported or if she was just checking to make sure Kayla was telling the truth. Then she wondered why she thought that.

The event that night was a movie. Maggie was kind of disappointed when she found out it was the story of David from the Bible. But it turned out okay; it was kind of interesting and they had popcorn, real popcorn cooked on the stove, with butter on it. Best of all, like at supper, they were allowed to sit with their friends. After the movie, the lady named Beth, asked some questions about the story and different kids answered them.

Kayla scooted her chair closer to Maggie's and whispered in her ear. "Which one is your boyfriend, Danny or David"

Maggie glared at her. "Neither! We don't have boyfriends and all that stuff. We're just a bunch of friends."

Kayla just nodded. "Good. I think I'll go after Danny."

Maggie could feel fire about to come out of her eyes. And she could feel her hand close into a fist. Why that … that …

And then she remembered that Jesus loves Kayla.

And she was supposed to too.

On Sunday they had breakfast in their cottages and then went to the Clubhouse and had a church service. Beth led the singing, some hymns like at her church, and some praise music like at David's church. The background music was on tape and the words on a screen. After the music, Brian gave a short message.

The message was based on the story of Ruth in the Bible, how she was a Moabitess, an outsider, not from Israel, how she and her Jewish mother-in-law, Naomi, were both widowed and had no one to help them get food or shelter. But Boaz was related to Naomi's husband and by Jewish law someone related to her husband should take care of his widow. Boaz became the kinsman redeemer, which means he bought back the land her husband left when he went to Moab. And Boaz ended up marrying Ruth. Then Bryan told them how this is a preview of what Jesus was going to do when He came - He would redeem not only the Jews but the Gentiles.

After the service they had lunch, just sandwiches and chips and salad. And they all went back to their cottages until supper. It wasn't a very exciting day to Maggie. And she knew part of it was because of Kayla.

But Monday was different.

Maggie fell in love at first sight. He was coal black with only a small white moustache on his upper lip and two small white stockings, one on a front and one on a back foot. His name was Deuce.

The stable held six horses and she was assigned to Deuce. She would be with him the entire two weeks of camp. If she stayed the second week, of course.

Patty showed the others by demonstrating with Maggie and Deuce how to stand safely with horses.

"Never stand behind a horse. Unless you want to take a chance on your head being kicked!" They all laughed nervously. "Stand to the side and keep your hand on them at all times, on the withers – that's a shoulder in people language."

Deuce lowered his head after he'd been assigned to Maggie and while Patty was pairing up the other horses and students. Maggie parted his forelock and rubbed his head. Then she stroked his neck and he lowered his head a little more. It was like he knew they belonged together.

"Do you see what Maggie is doing with Deuce?" Patty's voice pulled Maggie out of her silent bonding time with the horse.

"She just did the exact things that bond a horse to you. A mother horse, a mare, strokes the colt's neck, so that is a good way to show love to a horse." Patty walked over to them.

"At first glance, you might think Deuce is all black, except for a few white spots on his nose and feet. But if you look closely at his mane, you can see the brown at the tips. This is called a 'mixed mane' but it is considered black."

Danny was the only other person in their home club who signed up for the horseback riding lessons. She was surprised that they were put in the same class. No one she knew, except Kayla, was in her other class - Biblical Healing. Danny's horse was a chestnut colored mare, named Herself. Maggie wondered if the horse was named that because she thought her way was right all the time. She hoped not because Danny was really nervous about taking horseback lessons. And Maggie admitted that she'd talked him into it. She hoped maybe when they got home there'd be some time they could ride horses together. After all, Danny was her best friend, well Danny and Gretchen. She guessed she had two best friends.

They spent most of the first two hour class getting to know what the stables were like and how to care for the horses. They learned how to hold the lead, never ever to wrap it around their hand or they could get a rope burn. They had to hold it about twelve inches out and in a way that they could let go if the horse took off. That time was also to let the horses get used to the kids.

They learned how to put the saddle on, with help from the instructor and the two men who were her assistants. Maggie thought they looked just like cowboys out of the old movies. Finally the last fifteen minutes, just as Maggie thought she couldn't stand it any longer, they mounted the horses and were led around the fenced in barn lot outside the stable. Patty called it an enclosed riding arena.

Maggie thought it was the most exciting thing she'd ever done in her life.

A wagon filled with bales of hay, and pulled by a tractor, drove up to the gate. It was the same wagon, and tractor driver, that had brought them here from the main building where they all met for classes. It looked like something to take a hay ride in. Danny had made Maggie laugh on the way over by saying "This IS a hayride cause we're getting covered with hay while we ride."

All six of the kids taking lessons turned to Patty and thanked her and said good-bye to her and the two men.

Maggie looked longingly at Deuce and she thought he was sorry to see her go too.

Maggie was the last to go through the gate and was surprised by something bumping her shoulder from behind.

It was Deuce. She reached up and petted his nose just as Patty came running up to him.

The instructor was laughing. "I never saw him do this before. Maggie, you must have really won Deuce's heart. He's never tried to follow me out the gate!"

Maggie couldn't swallow the lump in her throat so she just nodded. Deuce sure had won her heart too.

"So how'd you like it?" Maggie finally turned to her friend when the wagon turned a corner in the road and she couldn't see the horse anymore.

Danny grinned. "It was better than I thought. I'm glad you talked me into it. Horses are neat, aren't they?"

Maggie nodded.

The other four kids were climbing on the haystacks, even though the guy driving the wagon had told them to sit still and not do that. Danny looked at Maggie and shrugged his shoulders.

She whispered, "Should we say anything?"

"We'd just make them mad."

"But if they got hurt, it would be our fault." She looked up at Buster, the tractor driver, but the noise of the tractor kept him from hearing anything, even the laughter from the climbers.

Danny nodded. He stood up and yelled back to the other kids. "Sit down, you might get hurt!" Just then the tractor made a turn and Danny tumbled over the side of the wagon.

Oh no! What could she do to make Buster stop? Was Danny hurt? It was all her fault for making him say something to the others.

But just then Buster looked back, and evidently saw there were only five of them. He pulled over to the side and turned off the noisy machine.

"What happened?"

Maggie swallowed hard but couldn't seem to make herself talk. So she stood up and pointed back toward where Danny lay on the ground.

Buster leaped down from the tractor and ran back to Danny. By the time he got there, Danny was sitting. She watched as the man helped her friend stand up. Danny seemed to be fine. That was a relief!

"What happened?" Buster frowned at Danny.

"Uh..." The other four kids were watching Danny and their wide eyes showed the fear that he would tell on them. Danny looked up at them in the wagon.

He turned to Buster. "I didn't pay attention to your rule and stood up. My fault."

The other kids smiled and two of the boys helped Danny climb up into the wagon. The one other girl looked at Maggie and smiled again.

She guessed they had made friends by not telling on them.

"Well, let it be a lesson to you..." And Buster got back on the tractor and took off toward the Clubhouse.

Chapter Seven

Frustration and Fury

Buster didn't report Danny's disobedience and Maggie was glad. It would have been really hard for her to keep her mouth shut and not take up for him. But at supper that night, she didn't keep her mouth shut. She told the home club kids, and Kayla, what Danny had done. "I think those other kids really respected him for that, too. You know, that he didn't tattle on them."

Kayla leaped up from her seat and ran around behind Danny's chair, put both arms around him and hugged. "What a hero! I guess we're both heroes now, huh Danny? Me yesterday and you today."

Maggie watched her friend's face turn red. David stood up.

"I think Jesus is the only real hero. And when we let Him work through us, He does good things." He picked up his tray. "Anybody going for seconds?"

Danny looked relieved and picked up his own tray. "I'll go with you." He ducked away from Kayla who still stood behind his chair.

The meal was Italian and Maggie noticed that the boys had chosen red spaghetti sauce for their pasta. She took Alfredo for her own. She loved Northern Italian and was glad they were given the choice.

Kayla got her own tray and followed the boys up to the food line. Polly looked over at Maggie, but didn't say a word. Maggie didn't either because anything she could think of to say wouldn't be nice.

Maggie noticed the overweight girl had piled her plate with some of each. And lots of buttery garlic bread. But no salad.

That third night they stayed in their cottages and didn't go to the clubhouse for a movie or anything. Sarabeth told them they were going to have a sharing time and one of the staff would be coming to lead it. But first she wanted them to all go off alone with their folders and make a list of the questions they would ask Jesus if He was there in person to answer them.

Whitney, one of Maggie's roommates, asked if she could go outside to make her list. Sarabeth answered "Yes, as long as you stay right around the cottage. And stay alone so you can think better." Whitney nodded and went to get her folder.

Mary Katherine curled up on one of the couches with her own folder.

That left the bedroom alone and Maggie smiled at Sarabeth. "I'll go to my room."

"I could go to your room too," Kayla said.

Sarabeth shook her head but said pleasantly, "No, you need to be off alone. And so does Maggie."

Kayla frowned and stomped off to her own room.

When Maggie closed the door behind her, she felt like she'd escaped. From what?

She fluffed up the pillows on her bed and added a blanket behind her to make it more comfortable. She picked up her folder and the pen that proclaimed *Fun To Be One Club* with the website address on it.

She tried to quiet her mind but all she could think of was how much Kayla irritated her. If only she hadn't told the girl about the camp! How dare she decide to "go after" Danny as a boyfriend! Not that Danny would ever want Kayla as a girlfriend. Danny didn't want any of that boyfriend-girlfriend stuff. And if he did, he sure wouldn't want that bragging fat pig!

Uh Oh. Jesus didn't like her calling Kayla that. *But it's true!*

"I'm sorry." She whispered. And maybe she was sorry – at least sorry she felt like she did. She clicked the pen and put it on the paper. "What would I ask You if You were right here in person?"

She thought back on the times at their own Clubhouse. "But Jesus, You are right here in person." She wished she was at the chicken coop so she could hear Him better – or at least have David or Danny or some of the others to help her hear Him.

She wrote, "Why can't I hear You here at camp?" But then she scratched it out. She knew why. Her mind was so filled up with irritation and disappointment about Kayla that, with the exception of the horseback riding lessons, she would rather not be there. She'd rather be home with Celie. The thought of her little sister and the way she'd hugged Maggie and said, "We miss you when you're not here," brought tears to her eyes.

What would she ask Jesus if He was standing here in His resurrected body?

"Would you please lay hands on my sister Celie and tell Leukemia to leave, and make her well?" She wrote it down. It was all she could think of except "Could you please make Kayla go away so camp could be fun?" And she knew she couldn't say that out loud in front of the others.

And she couldn't really say it to Jesus, cause she knew He had sent Kayla here to help her know about Him.

And she knew she shouldn't be mad at Jesus 'cause it seemed like He cared more about Kayla than her.

It was Beth and Brian who came to hold their meeting. Maggie was glad because she didn't have a class with them but wished she did. They were really friendly and she wanted to get to know them better.

When they were all seated around on the couches and chairs and the floor, Brian stood up in front of the table.

"Did all of you get your list of questions written?"

They all raised their hands but Kayla was the first one to speak. "I did!"

He nodded. "That's good. Let me ask you something. Did anybody have any questions they would have asked Jesus if it was just you and Him, and not a group meeting?"

Maggie felt her cheeks grow warm but she had, so she raised her hand. She noticed Whitney did too, and she smiled at her roommate who smiled back.

Brian nodded. "That's good too. That shows you were really thinking about what you really want to know."

Kayla said, "Well, I did too; I just didn't raise my hand."

Maggie's cheeks grew warm again, this time from embarrassment for Kayla. Couldn't the girl see how, how, inappropriate – Maggie could almost hear David supply the word – she acted?

Beth stood up then and smiled out at all of them. "Are we ready to share? Let's pray first. Lord, we are here together and asking You to speak to us. We have lots of questions and we want to know the answers. In Jesus Name, Amen.

"Now first of all I have a question that I want you to ask yourselves, but don't say the answer out loud. Ask yourself

'Do I have a personal relationship with Jesus or do I just believe in the history about Him?' "

Everybody was quiet for a few minutes, most with their eyes closed. Maggie didn't have to think about it; she knew she had a personal relationship with Jesus. But she looked over at Kayla. Uh Oh! Kayla didn't have her eyes closed and was looking at Maggie with her eyes narrowed. Maggie closed her own eyes and waited 'til Beth spoke again.

"Okay. Now if the answer was 'No, I just believe in what I've been taught about Him' I'd like for you to talk to me before I leave, okay? Now, who would like to ask the first question?"

Kayla raised her hand. "I would." When Beth nodded for her to go ahead, she read from her paper, "What makes your religion better than any other. What makes yours better than Buddha?"

There was silence for what seemed like a long time. Then Beth said, "Okay girls, does anybody have an answer for Kayla's question?"

Mary Katherine raised her hand. "Because Buddha didn't die for your sins." All the other girls nodded. Maggie was still staring at Kayla, who had a smirk on her face. Did she come here just to cause trouble? Did the devil send her instead of God sending her like Maggie had thought?

Beth agreed. "There are a lot of religions in this world. And some of them have some good standards to live by. Buddhism is one of those. It teaches love and kindness. And that is wonderful. But people don't have the nature to always be loving and kind. Humans needed a Savior and Jesus came to take all the old nature away from us and give us God's own nature of love.

Does that answer your question…what is your name?"

"Kayla. But how do we know that Jesus died for our sins?"

"Girls?" Beth looked out at the group.

This time Whitney spoke up. "The Bible says so."

But Kayla quickly answered her. "The Bible! There are a lot of ancient books. What makes the Bible so special?"

Maggie couldn't stay quiet any longer. "Because the Bible is alive. The Words are given by God and He comes to be with us when we read it and explains them and makes them come alive for us!" She looked right at Kayla. "If you read it, you'll see!"

Beth asked, "Kayla, have you ever read any of the Bible?"

For once Kayla was silent. She just shook her head.

Beth looked up at the clock. "Kayla, I really would like to talk to you sometime. You have some very good questions."

Kayla smirked again. Maggie couldn't believe her. Did she really think she had impressed anybody?

Beth asked, "Who else has a question they don't mind sharing with the group?"

Whitney raised her hand. When Beth nodded at her, she read, "Why do You let some people do bad things?"

"Anybody?"

A girl from one of the other bedrooms, a girl with brown pigtails, raised her hand.

"Because the Lord is a Shepherd, not a Zoo Keeper."

They all laughed.

Beth said, "I think I know what you mean..." She looked at Sarabeth. "Don't we have some nametags in the drawer over there?"

Sarabeth went and pulled out the tags and some markers. She passed them out and soon everybody had their names stuck on their tops.

Beth went on. "I think what Brittany meant was that God leads us and we choose whether to follow. He doesn't put us in cages so we can't do anything wrong. Does that answer your question, Whitney?"

The pretty blonde girl nodded but Maggie could tell she wasn't really satisfied with the answer.

Maggie raised her hand. "Isn't it because God gave man free will? I mean He told Adam not to eat the fruit of the tree of knowledge of good and evil. But He didn't … umm…He didn't put an electric fence around it or anything."

Everybody laughed again.

Beth said, "You're right, Maggie. Every person in this world has free will. We choose whether to follow the Shepherd," she nodded at Brittany. "Or whether to go off on our own."

Brian moved in closer to Beth. "The thing is, a lot of people don't know the Shepherd. They don't know the Words of Life. So they don't even know they are choosing wrongly. They are just doing what comes naturally to a fallen nature, a nature that is no longer connected with God."

Maggie saw Whitney nod. She was glad that helped her. Whitney seemed like a really nice girl though she was very quiet.

Kayla didn't raise her hand. "You mean you all believe all that stuff about Adam and Eve and a talking snake and all that?"

Again, silence filled the room. Finally Beth laughed, a funny little laugh.

"Yes, Kayla, I guess we all do."

Chapter Eight

Hope and Fury

Maggie watched as the guy began plucking the guitar strings. Then he started singing. She'd never heard the song. It wasn't the kind they sang at her church, but she liked it.

And she'd never seen anyone perform exactly like Michael Hernandez did. It was like the rest of them were not really in the room. He was singing to God about worshipping Him for who He is. And it was obvious that Michael knew who God is. Amy had introduced him and said that he was going to sing before he talked to them about healing.

It was the second day of the Biblical Healing Class and Maggie hoped she would learn something to help Celie. The first day, Amy and Gary - it still felt weird to call older people by their first names but - said Paul and Peter and James and John didn't use titles so they didn't either. The couple gave them a lot of Bible verses that showed definitely that God wanted to heal. Maggie was glad to know that. But she wanted to know how to get Him to do it!

She hadn't gotten to ask her question last night at the cottage because they ran out of time. Beth and Brian said they'd be back on Thursday night. There were other things scheduled for Wednesday.

Kayla was also in the class. Sarabeth either hadn't stopped Kayla from watching what Maggie wrote down on her class sign up sheet, or the girl really wanted to know about healing. Maggie didn't look at her but she wondered how her pen pal was reacting to the musical worship. She hoped the girl wasn't glaring like she did sometime when people were talking.

When Michael finished singing, he put the guitar against the wall and looked at the class for the first time. "Let's pray."

He bowed his head and so did Maggie. She guessed the rest of them did too.

"Father, thank you for loving us so much. Thank you for Who You Are. And that You never change. You are the same yesterday, today, and forever. We see You in Jesus and know that it is always Your will to heal. And always, we can trust You."

A thought flew into Maggie's mind about the little brother of a schoolmate back in second grade. The boy had been on his tricycle and rode it into the street. His mother went screaming after him but it was too late. A car hit him and he was killed immediately. How could that family trust Jesus?

She bit her lip and made her hands relax. When she looked up at Michael Hernandez, he was looking at her. With kindness in his eyes, like he knew what she was thinking.

"Sometimes it seems like it's hard to trust God. But that's because we forget that He's not in control of everything that happens in this world. We live in a fallen world, filled with sin and sorrow and sickness and accidents because of mankind re-belling against God. But when we know Him, and have faith in Him, and claim the promises He makes for our very own, we can trust that He will come through for us.

Maggie knew that. Why did she forget sometimes? Why, she'd said it just last night and then all she could think of today was that little boy and his family.

"I'd like to share a little with you about why I love music so much, why I always praise Him with music before I share my testimony.

"I was born in 1977 in the state of Washington, not Washington D.C., but the state that's far out west and far north. I was born to a family of farm workers. I don't remember much before I was six years old. Probably because life was soundless to me. Think about it. Everything was created with words, but I was born hearing impaired. I didn't know what sound was, what words were. I had a lot of operations, and I'm glad I don't remember them." He grinned and raised his eyebrows, and they all laughed.

"But finally one day, not too long after my last operation, I was in the kitchen with my Mom. She was cooking. I remember a wooden floor and an island in the middle of the kitchen. My Mom had black hair and brown eyes just like me. And she loved to cook and sing. That day the radio was on and for the first time sound happened to my ears, to me. And that sound was music. What an awesome thing. Think about it. Silence, silence, silence, all your life silence, and then music!!! It's still awesome to me.

"Then I could begin to learn to talk, listening to words and repeating them. I spent my elementary school years at the back of the classroom with a speech therapist, working on reading and writing skills. And speaking skills. It was so embarrassing! I mumbled when I talked and was always afraid of being laughed at by friends - and family. So mostly I kept to myself."

Maggie couldn't imagine how awful that would be. She'd never really thought about being grateful for hearing or speaking. It was just something everybody did. But that wasn't true.

Everybody didn't. She was so lucky. She could almost hear David's voice correcting her, *Not lucky - blessed!* But what about people who couldn't hear or speak? Why didn't God bless them? She forced her attention back to the front of the room.

"I spent a lot of time praying for God to help me. I cried in church parking lots, I wrote down my deep thoughts. I wanted God to hear the cries of my soul. Sometimes I thought God didn't hear me. I knew He could hear but thought He just wasn't listening. But now I know He was always there, guiding me, sending the help I needed.

"And He gave me a gift. It might not sound like a gift but it was. It was the gift of a burning desire to succeed, the gift of pushing myself toward a goal. Once I learned to read and communicate, I never stopped reading, never stopped pushing forward. I was the first in my immediate family to complete high school and then I went on to college and got a Bachelor's Degree in Psychology."

That reminded Maggie of a Kingdom Tale story from their clubhouse, 'The Prince and His Well.'

He grinned at them. "But I admit, my greatest love is music. It was the first thing I heard and to me it was the voice of God." He looked over at Amy. "Have I taken too long?"

She shook her head and smiled. "Take all the time you want."

He looked back at the class. "One of the things, other than music, that I get the most joy from, is talking to kids about possibilities. Nothing is impossible with God, and with God all things are possible. The Bible tells us so. I've been able to talk to troubled kids who had no hope for the future. Now you guys probably aren't troubled kids, and I'm sure you have a lot of hope for the future. But most of us can still use the encouragement. This is a class on healing and I believe in physical healing. It can happen miraculously instantly, or helped along by doctors, both were what mine was like. But also one of the most important kinds of healing is the healing of the self image. If we can get where we see ourselves as God sees us, the future is unlimited!"

Michael turned away but then turned back to them. "Let's pray again. 'Father, You have some beautiful children here, but not all of them see themselves as wonderful as You see them, forgiven, cleaned by the Blood of Jesus, and empowered by Your Holy Spirit. Lord, lead them to the mirror of Your Word and show them Yourself and themselves. In Jesus Name.'" He waited a long time before he finally said, "Amen."

During the silence, before the Amen, Maggie saw a picture in her mind of herself touching Celie and saying "Be healed." And she could see pink flooding Celie's pale face and a smile on Celie's lips. All things are possible with God, and nothing is impossible.

She realized the others were clapping for Michael Hernandez and she joined them. She glanced over at Kayla and was surprised to see the girl clapping very enthusiastically. With a big smile on her face!

Supper was hamburgers and fries and veggies and dips. And they didn't go back to their cottages after supper. Amy said that by the fourth night everybody was kind of tired so they'd go ahead and have the program and go to bed a little earlier. That suited Maggie just fine. She was tired. And disappointed.

On the walk back to the cottage after class, she'd asked Kayla, "So you really liked what Michael Hernandez said?"

The girl looked over at her with a look that said, 'you must be crazy.'

"I didn't even pay attention to what he said. But is he ever a hunk? Weren't you just drooling?"

Maggie didn't even answer her.

That night the gathering at the Clubhouse was music. Michael and a gospel quartet called The Patriots, and Beth and Brian were the performers, well the leaders. They all had different styles. Sometimes they performed and sometimes they got the kids to sing along with them. When they did that, the words were flashed on a screen to their right, just like at church.

Maggie loved the music, all of it. Especially she liked to sing along. She was surprised to see a lot of the kids raising their hands, just like at David's church, the one Danny and his Mom went to with Coach sometimes. People at her church didn't do that. She thought it would feel good but she'd never gotten the nerve to do it. Neither had Danny but he told her about it. Maybe while they were here…wow! Up went Danny's hands. Okay, she could do it too, if he could. So up went her hands.

They felt kind of silly and stiff at first. She remembered Danny saying that somebody told him to picture yourself saying to Jesus, "I surrender." But that felt stupid to her. She wasn't an outlaw. Then a picture came to her of when the twins were little and in a play pen. When Maggie walked in the room, they would hold their hands up for her to pick them up and hold them in her arms. That made sense. Her arms relaxed and she thought "Hold me, Jesus." And it felt good.

When the song ended, she looked around to see if anyone had been watching her.

Kayla stood there looking from her to Danny with arms crossed, shaking her head.

The fury rising inside Maggie made her feel like an outlaw after all!

Chapter Nine

Why Does God Allow...

"Just make it through this class," Maggie kept reminding herself during Biblical Healing on Wednesday morning. She couldn't keep her mind focused on what Amy and Gary were saying. She'd already decided she was going to join Whitney and Mary Kathryn for lunch, and the clubhouse kids could entertain Kayla by themselves. Last night was the last straw for her with her pen pal.

On the way back to the cottage after the music, Kayla had said, "You all really get into this praise stuff, don't you? It looks silly to me."

WWJD? What would Jesus do? Maggie wished David was there to react to Kayla. He would know what Jesus would do. Why didn't God put Kayla with him instead of her? She just wanted to slap the girl.

Finally she said the only words that came to her mind. "I'm sorry."

Kayla stopped walking and grabbed Maggie's arm. "What do you mean, you're sorry?"

Maggie hesitated only a few seconds before she jerked her arm away and walked on. The other girl could catch up with her if she wanted. And she did.

"What do you mean, you're sorry?" Kayla repeated.

What do I mean, Lord? "I'm sorry you don't know Jesus. I'm sorry you don't know how much He loves you. I'm sorry you don't want to show love back to Him." If she'd stopped there it would have been okay, but she didn't.

"And I'm sorry you came to camp to spoil everything for me."

And Maggie stomped off and left her standing there.

Kayla hadn't spoken to her since. She'd even taken a seat across the room in class this morning instead of right next to Maggie as usual. But this morning at breakfast, she had been her usual obnoxious self, reminding everyone of how she had saved Gretchen's life, and telling them how she'd found a cross necklace last night that one of her roommates lost.

Maggie thought Kayla probably hid it so she could be a hero again.

"What keeps us from receiving from God?" Amy's voice broke through the thoughts rambling around Maggie's mind.

"That's one of the most important questions we can ask. We've talked about – and seen in the Bible – that it's always God's will to heal. So why don't we always see healing?"

Maggie nodded. That's it – why don't we? She really needed to pay attention now and not miss anything.

Amy picked up the Bible. "I believe this is one of the most important things we can ever learn – in any area, not just healing. Without putting this into practice we can't receive anything from God. Does anybody have any idea what I'm talking about?"

A boy raised his hand. "Faith. The Bible says that without faith we can't please God."

Amy nodded. "That's true. Good answer. We have to believe God's promises or we won't receive them. But that isn't
what I'm talking about right now. This is something that even
if we know God's will and even if we believe His promises, if
this isn't done, we won't receive." She looked around the
room. "Anybody else?"

Nobody said anything.

Amy began to read. "Therefore I say to you, What things
you desire, when you pray, believe that you receive them, and
you shall have them."

The same boy interrupted her. "But isn't that faith – believing you receive them when you ask Him?"

Amy smiled. "Yes, but the verse goes on. Oh, I'm reading
from Mark 11:24 and 25. 'And when you stand praying, forgive, if you have anything against anybody, so that your Father
also which is in heaven may forgive you your trespasses.'" She
looked up and smiled at them. "Now, anybody see it?"

Forgive. Most of the kids said it out loud. "Forgive!"

"Right," Amy said. "We have to learn to forgive. And tomorrow we're going to look at what forgiveness is, and how to
practice it."

*Oh great! First I'm going to keep Celie from getting healed
by not having faith and now by my unforgiveness of Kayla. But
how can I forgive? I don't want to be friends with her. I ...
well, I really think I hate Kayla.*

Whitney and Mary Kathryn acted thrilled that Maggie
joined them for lunch. They told her about their classes. Mary
Kathryn was taking Become All God wants You to Be, and
Beth and Brian were her teachers.

"They are really, really good. I know I was wrong and even
people in my church don't believe this way but I had it in my
head that if you really love God you become a priest or a nun.

But I really see it now, how God can call you to be … well anything. Like, my Mom for instance. She's an awesome Mom. God made her to be a Mom and He made my Dad to be a dentist. They aren't, how did they say it? Oh, they aren't second class citizens in the Kingdom of God just because they aren't in a professional ministry like a priest or something."

Maggie nodded. "I hadn't thought about it, but you know probably a lot of people think that way – second class citizens in the Kingdom." She turned to Whitney.

"And what class are you in?"

Whitney smiled her shy smile. "I'm in Shaun and April's class. We're learning how to study the Bible. I really like it. Today was our third day and so far we've looked at an overview of what God did in the Old Testament in order to get to the New Testament. And the word Testament really means Covenant. They make it interesting. And what about your class?"

Maggie looked down. "I'm taking Biblical Healing. But it's more complicated than I thought."

Mary Kathryn put down her soup spoon. The homemade potato soup was completely gone from her bowl. "What do you mean?"

"Well, I'm not sure. I thought I'd learn how to make everybody well. But, well, we've found out that God wants to heal. But He does it different ways. You remember Michael, the guy that sang last night?"

Both girls nodded.

"He spoke to the class yesterday and told us he had lots of operations before he got healed. But the healing happened in his home, all of a sudden - like a miracle. And today we talked about faith, believing God's promises. And…and other stuff."

Whitney and Mary Kathryn were looking at her like they were waiting for her to go on.

"Forgive. We're going to talk more about it tomorrow but Amy says we have to forgive before we can receive from God." Maggie sighed. "And right now I'm not sure I can, or even want to, forgive somebody."

Whitney nodded. "Oh, I know what you mean, Maggie. I really know."

Mary Kathryn just looked at them. Maggie could tell she wasn't really struggling to forgive anybody. Lucky girl ... uh, blessed girl.

That afternoon Maggie forgot about forgiveness and Kayla and Celie and everything for the two hours she spent with Deuce. Everything fled away into the background as she learned how to make her horse, and she thought of him as her horse now, walk certain ways. They had learned several things like walk and trot. Today they were learning to get the horses to canter. Patty said that by next week they would learn to lope and gallop.

She was quiet on the ride back in the wagon. Danny was talking to some of the other guys. They'd become friends with him since that first day when he didn't tattle on them. Maggie wondered if her parents would buy Deuce for her. They'd have to buy a lot or something out in the country to keep him on. And she'd have to go out every day to feed him. And take care of him. And... the bubble popped. No way. But how could she stand to leave him in, how many days? Ten if she stayed til a week from Saturday, three if she left this Saturday.

She wanted to be there for Celie, and she sure wanted to get away from Kayla. But how could she leave Deuce?

At dinner it was announced that tonight was game night. They would have lots of board games and card games and games like Charades. Everyone would be able to choose what kind of games they would play. And they could switch around and play several. Again, they wouldn't go back to their cottages after supper but stay and begin playing right after they ate. And dessert would be served about an hour and a half later. But the games would last longer than the music did last night. They all had to stay the whole time unless they got special permission for some good reason and their Senior was willing to go back to the cottage with them.

Maggie couldn't really decide what game she wanted to play so she just kind of walked around and watched some of the others. Danny and David were playing a board game with two of the boys from riding class. Ray was in the charade group. It was kind of funny really. These days most kids played games on an ipad or smart phone or something but they weren't allowed to bring that kind of stuff to camp. Maggie guessed it was because they wanted them to interact with each other. She wandered over to where Gretchen and Polly were seated with some other girls.

"Hey Maggie! We're playing Crazy Eights. Come on and join us."

Maggie hadn't got to spend any time with Gretchen since they'd come to camp. Or Polly either. They didn't have any classes together. And of course they weren't in the same cottage. Lunch and supper was the only time they were together and then the rest of the group – and Kayla – were there.

She smiled at them. "No, I think I'll just watch for now. Maybe later."

She saw Sarabeth standing against the wall and walked over to her. "Do we have to play a game or can we just watch?"

"It's okay to just watch. But don't you want to play?"

Maggie shook her head.

"Are you okay?"

Maggie felt tears leap into her eyes. She bit her lip. And looked at the older girl. "Not really."

"Would you like to go back to the cottage and talk?"

Would she? She didn't think so. Anything she talked about would just be gossiping about Kayla. Or telling how scared she was about Celie. She shook her head.

"Not now. Thanks anyway." She didn't look at Sarabeth again but turned and went to the Girls Restroom.

Just as she opened the door, she heard a familiar voice, and stopped.

"Yeah, Maggie and I used to be good friends but then she got kind of wild. She's always trying to get Danny and David to pay attention to her. You know, the ones she usually sits at the table with? Well, any boy really. I feel kind of sorry for her but I just don't spend as much time with her as I used to."

Maggie couldn't believe her ears. She closed the door quietly and moved away. In a few minutes Kayla came out of the restroom with one of their cottage mates, a girl named Kathy who went to the Presbyterian Church. Maggie pretended to be watching a board game until they passed by her.

Now what was she supposed to do about that?

But just then, Whitney came up and touched her arm. "Maggie, could I talk to you?"

"Sure. Where?"

"The girls restroom?"

They went in and sat on the couch right inside the door.

"If anybody comes in, I'll stop talking," Whitney whispered.

Maggie nodded. And she'd watch the door so if anybody opened it and didn't come in, like she had, she could warn Whitney.

"You remember when Beth and Brian came to the cottage

the other night?"

"Sure."

"I asked why God let people do bad things."

Maggie nodded again.

"See, it's really awful at my house. Dad hits my Mom a lot. They don't go to church. I go on the bus. It's the church that paid for me to come to camp."

"I'm sorry about your Dad." One day Maggie was going to realize how lucky … blessed … she really was.

"My Mom is nice. She doesn't go to church because he won't let her. And I want to know what you think. I want her to get a divorce. Do you think that's wrong of me?"

"No. I'd want my Mom to get away from someone who hit her and wouldn't let her go to church too."

"Do you think it's okay to pray for that?"

Maggie thought a minute. "I don't know. I used to think divorce was always wrong but my friend Danny…well his Mom was divorced and then his Dad got nice and got married again and had another boy. And Danny's Mom met somebody and got married – just last Friday. And everything turned out good for everybody." She shrugged. "But I do know for sure that it's not God's will for your Mom to get hit and bossed around. So we can ask Him to get her out of that mess. Right?"

Whitney smiled. And nodded. "Would you pray?"

Maggie took Whitney's hand. "Father, we come to You to ask You to help Whitney's Mom not get hurt any more. And that she be able to go to church. We ask it in Jesus Name." Uh Oh. *When you stand praying, forgive if you have anything against anybody.* She looked at Whitney. "They said in my class today that when we pray we need to forgive so we can get what we ask from God."

Whitney's eyes opened wide. She frowned at Maggie. "What does it mean to forgive? Is that Forgive and Forget?"

Maggie shrugged. "I don't know. But we're supposed to find out more in class tomorrow. I'll let you know."

Whitney smiled. "Thanks, Maggie. And, he's really not my Dad, he's my stepfather. But he gets mad if I say that. He pretends that he's my real Dad."

"Where is your real Dad?"

"He died when I was a baby. I never knew him. Mom married Craig later." She laughed. "There I said it! Craig! He came around when I was about three years old and Mom called him Craig so I did too. But after they got married, he spanked me if I called him anything but Daddy. I don't know if I can ever forgive and forget all the stuff he's done."

Maggie felt that fire begin to rise up in her again. What was wrong with people like that? Like Craig … and Kayla?

Chapter Ten

What Forgiveness Isn't - Whew!

Maggie and Whitney left the restroom and found Gretchen and Polly who had just finished the game they were playing. The girls they'd been playing with decided to join a group playing charades, so Maggie and Whitney took their places and a new game of Crazy Eights was soon underway.

Whitney fit right in with her friends from home and they all laughed a lot. Gretchen told Whit – she said her Mom called her Whit when they were alone, and she liked it – about the Fun To Be One Club they'd started at home before they found out about the national one.

"That's really neat." Then Whitney frowned. "But what's all this other stuff? The Kingdom Project and King's Chapel and all that on the signs when we got here?"

Gretchen said, "I don't know."

Maggie added, "Mrs. Sanders, David's Mom, said that the Fun To Be One Club is just a part of a bigger project to get Christians of all ages to work together and love each other no matter what church or denomination they go to."

Polly nodded.

"And did you see that castle when we came in?" Whit sounded excited about the castle.

"Yeah, I'd almost forgotten. Do you think it's part of the Club, or the Project?" Maggie remembered thinking it looked a lot like Cinderella's castle at Disney World.

"Why don't we ask?" Gretchen looked around. "There's Sarabeth." She got up and went over to get the older girl.

When the two got back to the table, Sarabeth smiled at Maggie. "Ah, you found a game you wanted to play!"

Maggie nodded.

Gretchen sat back down and Sarabeth sat beside her. "What we want to know about is that castle we saw when we got here. Is it part of this whole thing – the Kingdom Project?"

Sarabeth smiled. "I wondered when someone was going to ask about that. Yes, it is. It's part of the … well, I don't know if I'm supposed to tell. Amy will tell everybody about it, let's see, tomorrow or the next day for sure. You can wait til then, can't you?"

The girls laughed and assured her that they could wait one more day, maybe two.

Amy didn't mention the castle at breakfast Thursday morning. But breakfast was a happy time for Maggie. Gretchen joined Maggie and Whitney and Mary Kathryn.

Maggie noticed that Ray and Danny were both at other tables too. That left David, Polly, Kyliegh, Scooter, and Harold at their old table – with Kayla! That was just like David to stay with Harold and Scooter. And like Polly to stay with Kyliegh. And like both of them to be nice to Kayla. Kayla's new friend, the one she told all the lies to about Maggie, was at the table too. And another girl was sitting by Kyliegh, probably the

Catholic girl she'd made friends with in her own cottage.

The girls talked about the castle and wondered if they'd get to go in it while they were there.

"I'd like to see that King's Chapel thing too. I wonder if the Retreat Center is a camp for adults like ours is for kids." Gretchen always wanted to see new things. That was one of the reasons Maggie liked her so much.

"When Amy tells us about the castle, why don't you ask her?" Maggie just remembered something. "Hey, Beth's coming to our cottage tonight. We could ask her then!"

Whit smiled. "I will!"

The girls separated from Gretchen to join Sarabeth for their walk back to the cottage. Gretchen joined her own Senior, Susie, and waved goodbye.

And Kayla joined them. Yuck. It had been almost two days since Kayla had spoken to Maggie. And Maggie was glad. She just wished Kayla wouldn't speak to anybody. God struck people blind in the Bible, maybe He would strike Kayla whatever it was called when you can't talk, dumb? She was already the other kind of dumb! Maggie could feel her fists tightening and her teeth clenching. Wasn't she in good shape to go to healing class? Oh yeah, and learn to forgive and forget? No way.

When their cottage group got to the Clubhouse, Maggie turned away from the others and walked as fast as she could toward the classroom, so Kayla couldn't catch up with her. She probably wouldn't anyway. She'd already told her roommate that she didn't hang around Maggie anymore. Because Maggie was so boy crazy. She could feel her teeth clenching again. It was all she could do to keep from going to that girl, Kathy, and telling her the truth. But something inside wouldn't let her do that. And Maggie knew Who that Something was. And she was a little bit mad at Him. He wouldn't let her say things. Why couldn't He stop Kayla from saying things too?

"Because I don't live in her. Yet."

A warm feeling flooded Maggie. It was the first time she'd heard His voice since "Go to Camp." And then it hit her. "Yet." He said "Yet." Did that mean that Kayla would become a Christian? Would she invite Jesus to live in her heart?

Maggie remembered how she'd prayed for that, how she had asked Jesus to let her help Kayla. She guessed that request still stood, even though she didn't want to help her anymore.

Maggie sighed. It was all too confusing for her. And she didn't think she could make herself like that girl no matter how hard she tried. But, if Jesus came to live in Kayla... well, she'd see.

Amy greeted the class and opened with prayer. "Today we are going to look at forgiveness – what it is and what it isn't. I want you to take notes, make a list. Because this is important."

What it isn't? That caught Maggie's attention. She thought she knew what forgiveness was. Excusing the person for doing something you didn't like, right?

"First of all, forgiveness is NOT excusing bad behavior." Amy grinned at them and laughed. "Isn't that a relief?"

Most of the class laughed too.

"To really forgive, you have to recognize the behavior as sin, as a wrong that God Himself doesn't like. You have to see it as a bad thing. You can't excuse bad things. You have to see them like God does. The one who does them deserves to be punished."

Whoa! That's pretty tough. Did she want Kayla punished for the things she'd done? She didn't really want anything bad to happen to the girl, except at the times she wanted to punch her in the face. But she didn't want God to do something bad to her. And God doesn't do bad things anyway. Does He?

Amy was talking again. "That's the main thing that Forgiveness isn't – it is NOT excusing the wrong. The second thing that Forgiveness isn't is saying that everything is okay now, like it never happened. You've heard that saying 'Forgive and Forget?'?"

Maggie could see that the others were nodding like she was.

"You are not ever going to really 'forget.' You will remember that it happened. God doesn't wipe out the memory cells in your brain and make you some kind of zombie!"

They all laughed.

"The memory will stay there, but the power of that memory to make you hate, to make you angry, to make you bitter toward the person, or to hurt you, won't be there anymore. Now that really gets into what Forgiveness IS, but I wanted to bring that part of what it isn't up now so you could see the difference between saying what the person did was okay, and just not having it be powerful in your emotions anymore."

Maggie nodded. She remembered one time when Cindy got mad and kicked her because she wouldn't give her a toy that she was afraid the twins would break when they were only two. The kick hurt her shin. It was a bad thing for Cindy to do. Mom had spanked Cindy's hand for doing it and made Cindy tell Maggie she was sorry. And Mom told Maggie to say "I forgive you." Now Maggie could remember that it happened, but she wasn't mad at Cindy any more. She nodded again.

"Another thing that Forgiveness is not is a restored relationship. Just because you forgive somebody does not mean you have to trust them again. And it doesn't mean you have to be friends with them."

THAT was a relief. She'd never wanted to be friends with Kayla in the first place. And she sure didn't want to be friends with her now that she knew what a liar she was besides being a braggart.

"But you do have to be nice to them. Just like you are supposed to be nice to everybody, because you are to walk like Jesus."

Okay, she guessed she could be nice to Kayla. Maybe. Someday. But it sure would be easier to just not be around her.

"Now – what Forgiveness IS! Are you writing these things down?

Oh, Maggie had forgotten. She guessed the others had too because Amy went over it again and gave them time to make their list.

Forgiveness is not excusing a wrong.

Forgiveness is not forgetting and saying it's okay now.

Forgiveness is not a restored relationship.

"Forgiveness IS seeing that the punishment for the sin was taken by Jesus on the cross."

That made Maggie sit up straight in her seat! Jesus was hurt on the cross because Kayla told lies about Maggie? Jesus was hurt on the cross because Maggie said she wished Kayla hadn't come to camp? That made her heart hurt.

"The second thing Forgiveness is, is putting the bad thing in the past. Like I said earlier, it doesn't mean forgetting but it means that when you send the sin to the cross, it can't affect your emotions any more. And there's another part of that too, a very exciting part. When you send the sin to the cross for Jesus to take and bear the punishment, He can wipe away all the effects of that from your life."

Maggie tried to think what that would mean. If she forgave Kayla for telling lies about her, then Kathy wouldn't believe Maggie was boy crazy? Or did it just mean that Maggie wouldn't care what Kathy thought?

"The third thing that Forgiveness is, is another very important part of putting the bad thing in the past. Forgiveness doesn't talk about the sin anymore."

Groan. That meant she couldn't even tell Kayla she knew about her lies. She'd already been good about not gossiping with her friends about the girl. But she couldn't even tell her what she thought?

Was she ready to forgive? She wasn't sure.

But would her unforgiveness stop Celie from getting healed? And stop Whit's Mom from getting free?

Chapter Eleven

Depression and Danger

That afternoon with Deuce wasn't as magical as it had been every other day. They learned how to take a hoof pick and clean the horses' hooves. You got the mud and rocks out so they couldn't hurt the horses feet.

Patty said "I want to show you how to tell if their frogs are healthy."

Maggie pictured Deuce with a frog on his shoulder – his wither – whispering in his ear, kind of like Jiminy Cricket did with Pinocchio. She couldn't help but smile.

Patty laughed. "I thought that would get you." She came over and lifted up Deuce's foot and pointed out a place behind the hard part. "This is called a frog." She motioned to the other kids to come closer. "See, Deuce has a very healthy frog. It's moist and not too dry. Go look and see if your horses have healthy frogs too."

Deuce seemed impatient. He sniffed a lot and threw his head back and wouldn't stand still. Maybe it was a good thing that Maggie couldn't take him home with her. She couldn't make him calm down.

Even Patty noticed. She came over and put her hand on Deuce's neck. "What's wrong, boy? Are you okay?" Maggie felt like she ought to tell the instructor it was all her fault. Deuce was probably picking up her bad mood.

They did get to ride again after they finished the grooming stuff but it just wasn't as much fun as before. She couldn't feel the bond with Deuce. She hoped it wasn't gone forever.

Danny had made such good friends with the other guys that he didn't pay any attention to Maggie either. Who needs any of them? Maggie wiped a tear away when they were in the wagon on the way back to the Clubhouse, and hoped no one noticed. They didn't. They were all too busy talking and having fun.

When they got back to the cottage, Sarabeth told them they wouldn't be going back to the Clubhouse for dinner that night.

Kayla asked the question for all of them. "Why not?"

Sarabeth sighed. "Well, there was an accident today. One of the kids that was taking canoeing fell in the water and had to be taken in to the hospital."

"Oh, no!" Nearly all the girls said the same thing at the same time.

Maggie felt a pain in her chest. Gretchen was taking the canoeing class. She tried to take a deep breath.

"C...can you tell us who it was?"

"I'm afraid I don't know. It was one of the boys in Cottage Five."

Then she could breathe again. But how ugly was that? Just because it wasn't Danny, who was with her in the afternoon class, or Gretchen, it was still somebody.

"Is he going to be okay?" Whitney asked in her soft voice.

"We don't know yet. Somebody did CPR on him and he was breathing but the staff nurse still felt like he should go be checked out."

The girls all nodded. Sarabeth went on. "They just decided that since tonight is Pizza night, it would be just as good to eat in our cottages."

"Pizza, yay!!!" Several of the girls voiced their approval.

Sarabeth grinned. "And it will be delivered, like at home!" Just then the Senior's cell phone buzzed and she answered it. "Sure. That would be great for us. Is it okay with the big guys?" She waited a minute. "Great! See you in a few."

"My friend Susie is bringing her group over – that's Cottage 3. They're going to eat with us."

"Are Beth and Brian still coming tonight?" Maggie knew Whitney asked because she wanted to know about the castle.

Sarabeth shrugged. "I don't know yet."

Maggie figured that they would have to contact the kid's parents. Maybe he would have to go home. She wondered how far away he lived. And for the first time it occurred to her to wonder how Kayla got there, all the way from Texas.

But since they weren't speaking, she couldn't ask.

In just a few minutes, a knock came on the cottage door and without waiting, it opened. Susie walked in, followed by her group. Gretchen broke away and ran toward Maggie, who could tell her friend had been crying.

What was wrong?

"Oh, Maggie! It was awful. Scooter fell out of the canoe. And when they pulled him back out of the water, it looked like he wasn't breathing. But Harold gave him mouth to mouth resuscitation and then he was for sure breathing."

"Scooter!" It never occurred to Maggie that it might be one of their boys. "Is he okay?"

"He says he's fine but Jon and the nurse decided to take him to the hospital anyway, just to make sure. His parents said that was okay."

"They called his parents?"

Gretchen nodded.

Susie said, "Anytime anything happens that could be dangerous or hurtful to you guys, we call the parents. But I was surprised that the other boy gave him mouth to mouth instead of Jon doing it." She and Sarabeth looked at each other with frowns.

"Oh it wasn't Jon's fault," Gretchen protested. "He's the best. But we were close to the shore and Harold just pulled Scooter out and was already doing his thing before Jon could get there."

Maggie saw Sarabeth and Susie look at each other again, this time obviously trying to not smile. She guessed it was the way Gretchen said Harold was 'doing his thing.'

"When will we know what the hospital said?" Maggie looked at Susie.

"Should be anytime n…" Just then the melody "Take Me Out To the Ballgame" sounded from Susie's jeans pocket. "Hello?" She nodded into the cell phone. "Great. See ya later." The Senior smiled and looked at Gretchen. "He's fine and will be staying at camp."

All the girls joined Maggie and Gretchen in cheering! Even Kayla.

"I'm hungry," she said. "When will the pizza get here?"

Maggie suddenly realized that she was hungry too. She hoped it would be soon.

Sure enough, another knock came on the door. This time a voice shouted. "Pizza anybody?"

All the girls yelled, "Yes!" And Brian came in carrying a stack of pizza boxes, only these boxes were plain and didn't have the name of a shop on them. Behind him was Beth with a large box in her arms.

"We decided that since we were coming here later anyway, we'd just bring the supper ourselves and eat with you." Beth laid the box on the table and Kayla immediately opened it. Without asking. Maggie wanted to shake her head and roll her eyes but she didn't. At least people didn't think they were good friends anymore.

Inside the box were two big bowls of salad and a bunch of bottles of salad dressings. And also some baskets covered with napkins but Maggie could see a breadstick peeking out of one end of a basket. Yay, even if she didn't like the pizza, she always loved breadsticks, and the ones the other night were great. She hoped … yes, there were sticks of butter on a plate, and it was so warm from the bread, the plate was filling up with melted butter.

"We brought enough for both cottages since they said you'd all be here." Beth looked over at Susie. "We'll just meet together tonight. On Monday we went to all three girls' cottages separately. We'll go on to Cottage 2 when we leave here." She laughed. "Next week the boys have to put up with us on Monday and Thursday nights!"

Brian led them in blessing the food and then, since there wasn't room at the table for all of them, not even half of them, they took their paper plates full of pizza and bread sticks, and paper bowls full of salad, and went to chairs and couches and the floor. Sarabeth and Susie sat on the floor and Maggie followed their example. All the girls waited until Brian and Beth sat down on the couch before taking any of the chairs. Kayla plopped down on the couch beside Beth.

"Oh shoot!" Beth said. "We forgot to bring the drinks."

"Be right back." Brian jumped up and went out the door.

Whitney said, "He's really a nice man."

Beth smiled at her. "Yes, he is. A really nice man."

Maggie wondered if Beth guessed that Whitney wasn't used to being around a nice man.

When Brian came back, he had large bottles of cola, generic, but still not just the lemonade and tea they'd had every other lunch and supper. He also brought in a bag of ice and plastic cups.

For a while everybody just ate and didn't talk. The pizza was good. Maggie was glad they had some that didn't have pepperoni; she didn't like pepperoni. And the bread sticks were awesome again. And there was bleu cheese dressing for her salad.

Whitney was the first to speak. "Beth, before we get started on our lesson or talk or whatever it is, can I ask you a question."

Beth laughed. "Sure. Can't guarantee I have the answer but you can ask."

"What about the castle? Are we going to get to see it?"

Maggie saw all the girls turn to look at Beth.

"Well..." Beth looked at Brian, who shook his head. "I have the answer but I'm not supposed to tell." She was quiet a minute. "Amy will be talking about that tomorrow. But I can tell you this, I think it's okay." She looked at Brian again and he just closed his eyes and shook his head again. "You won't be disappointed."

"Yes!" Whitney gave a thumbs up and several of the girls clapped.

When they had put all the trash in a huge black garbage bag and stored the leftovers in the refrigerator, they gathered back on the floor and chairs and couches. Beth and Brian sat at the table.

"Okay, do you all remember the question you were going to ask Jesus, if you didn't already get a turn on Monday?"

All twenty-two girls nodded, even those who had already asked their questions.

"Well, who wants to go next?"

Maggie felt a thumping inside her chest and felt like she

should ask her question. She raised her hand. But then she remembered that she wasn't supposed to let anybody know about Celie's sickness. Why hadn't she thought about that earlier? And Gretchen, from home, was here. She put her hand down really quick.

"Maggie?" Beth was looking at her.

"Umm. I think I changed my mind. Sorry." And she looked down at the floor. What an idiot she must seem to the other girls.

She felt Gretchen, who was sitting beside her on the floor, nudge her. When she looked up, her friend gestured 'what's wrong?' with her hands. Maggie just shook her head and looked away.

Nobody said anything and the thumping in Maggie's chest got louder. She raised her hand again. Beth smiled at her and nodded.

"Okay. I changed my mind because my parents told me not to tell anybody about this. But I know you guys won't say anything. None of you even know my family except Gretchen." She looked over at her friend. "And you won't tell, will you?"

Gretchen shook her head.

"My little sister has to go for a bone marrow test Monday. They are afraid she has Leukemia." She couldn't keep the tears from coming into her eyes. "If I could ask Jesus a question…if He were here in person, I'd ask Him to…" She took a deep breath. "Okay, I'll put it in a question to Him. I'd say, I do say, "Please, Jesus, will you make Leukemia leave my sister and heal her." Then she put her head down on her knees and let the tears flow onto her jeans.

Chapter Twelve

Shocked, Subdued, and Expectant

There was silence for several seconds. Maggie realized that Beth couldn't really ask the group what Jesus would answer, like she had the other night. Now what?

'What' was definitely NOT what Maggie expected. She heard a growl and looked up.

It was Kayla who stood up. "And do you know what Jesus would say? He'd say 'Sorry, can't help you' and he'd leave and walk away. If he was really there in the first place. I think people made him up to get our hopes up and then ... then cause us to be hurt more." And with that pronouncement Kayla stomped off, and really stomped so much that some pictures on the wall swayed from the stomping. The girl went to her bedroom and slammed the door.

Beth looked at Maggie and spoke in a soft voice. "Do you mind if I go talk to Kayla first? As strange as it seems, I think that she must be hurting even more than you are."

Maggie nodded. And Gretchen joined her arm with Maggie's while Beth headed toward the bedroom.

Brian said, "Maggie has asked Jesus a very important question but it's to do something, not to explain something, so I won't ask you what you think He would say. Unless some of you have something you want to share." He looked around at the group, who all looked very solemn and almost scared.

Maggie lifted her hand again. "I think I should say something. I believe with all my heart that Jesus wants to heal Celie - that's my sister. But I get afraid that my fears, and my sins, will stop Him from being able to do it." She looked around at the others.

Brian nodded. "Good, Maggie. That's honest. Now, does anyone think they know what Jesus might say to Maggie now?"

Maggie watched as the girls from both cottages stared at the floor. Nobody had a suggestion.

The silence continued.

Then suddenly Whitney's head came up. She looked at Maggie. Then she looked nervously at Brian. "Something came to my mind. Should I say it?"

Brian nodded. "Of course."

Whitney turned back to Maggie. "I really thought I heard that He would say *It will be okay. I have healed her and she will be fine.*" Then she looked at Brian again. "Was that okay?"

He smiled at her. "Yes. And we'll all agree that is true, okay?"

And they all said together "Okay!"

Maggie looked at Whitney in awe. And thought, *I wish I could hear Jesus like that.*

Brian smiled at her as if he knew what she was thinking. Then he spoke to the whole group. "People often think that when God talks they will hear a big booming voice or something. But that rarely happens. Most of the time when God speaks, it is like a thought that just comes to your mind." He turned to Whitney, "Was that what happened with you?

She nodded. "I was just looking at Jesus in my mind and then that thought came to me."

"That's it. You got one of the main keys to hearing Him. You were looking at Him with your mind, not trying to figure something out. When we quiet our own thoughts and look at Him, He can get through to us."

Just then Beth came out of Kayla's room and closed the door. "Kayla is going to stay in her room the rest of the night. And you girls need to be praying for her. She had a great disappointment a few years ago and it has colored her understanding of God. Pray with me?"

They all nodded and bowed their heads.

"Father, You love Kayla very much but she doesn't know it. Please show her who You really are. We ask in Jesus Name, as His body in the earth. Amen."

The rest of the evening was more subdued than any of the meetings at the Fun To Be One Club camp had ever been. The few questions for Jesus that were asked were pretty boring, like "How do you know if somebody's been born again?" and "What is the worst sin?" The only fun thing that happened was when one of the girls from Whitney's cottage asked, "Jesus, do people still have to go to the bathroom in heaven?" And everybody giggled.

Nobody had an answer to that but Beth was obviously trying to mask a grin when she announced that it was time for her and Brian to be moving on.

They all hugged the two good-bye and after they left, the girls got out some games and played for a while.

Finally Maggie couldn't stand it anymore. "I think the answer is 'no'."

"What?" Several of the girls spoke at once.

"I don't think we have to go to the bathroom in heaven."

Sarabeth and Susie both laughed. Sarabeth asked "Why?"

"I think there we just eat and drink what our new bodies need and absorb, so there's no waste to come out."

Susie replied, "Sounds good to me. That must have been Jesus' answer, right?" And she looked at Sarabeth.

The other girl just shook her head and rolled her eyes toward heaven. But Maggie could see her smiling.

Toward the end of breakfast, Danny asked Maggie if they could talk. They pulled their chairs to an empty table that napkins and ketchup and stuff were kept on.

"I need to talk to you," he said. "I'm not feeling very Christian these days. I'm not sure coming to camp has been good for me."

Maggie laughed. "I know what you mean! I feel the same way. But what's your problem?"

Danny looked surprised but he told her. "Harold is a big hero now since he saved Scooter's life. But I'm still suspicious of him. And feel guilty for thinking that Harold's main motive was to be a hero. He reminds me of the night that Kayla girl unchoked Gretchen and then bragged about it. I hate being judgmental. That's a big sin, just as bad as being prideful. And I've asked myself if I'm jealous that Harold had saved somebody's life instead of me. But I really don't think so."

Maggie frowned. "Of course you aren't jealous! And I feel the same way you do - about both Harold and Kayla." She hesitated before she went on. "Especially Kayla. Danny, I overheard her telling lies about me. And I wanted to choke her." She hesitated again. "And I found myself calling her ugly names in my mind."

It was Danny's turn to laugh. Then he sobered. "I shouldn't laugh but I don't blame you. And to be honest, the way she acts to me makes me do the same thing."

Maggie joined him as they both laughed.

But then they stopped as the main object of their laughter came over to their table.

"Hi, Danny." Kayla smiled. Then she said "Hi, Maggie" in a totally different voice, without looking at her penpal.

"What do you need, Kayla?" Danny asked.

"Nothing, just thought I'd join you two."

"Well if you don't mind," he said, "We're having a serious discussion about sin and we'd rather be alone."

Kayla's eyes narrowed and she turned to Maggie with a smirk. "I understand." and she walked away.

Maggie couldn't help but laugh this time. "Danny, I think you might have worded that a little differently. The way that girl thinks, she'll probably be spreading the word that you and I were planning to sin together."

His mouth dropped open. "Oh my gosh, you're right. I never thought about that." He shook his head. "I'm sorry."

Maggie laughed again. "You know that was probably a good thing. Now that I don't feel alone in my judgmental thoughts, it makes me care less about what she thinks - or says. We'll just trust the Lord with our reputations, right?"

Danny nodded and even managed a small smile. "Right. Let's pray, okay?" Then he laughed. "But we won't hold hands when we pray."

That brought a horse laugh from Maggie and she noticed several kids from nearby tables looking at her.

Danny prayed. "Lord, we hold up first of all ourselves. We don't want to be judgmental or critical so please help us to love the way You love. And forgive the way you forgive. And Lord, help Kayla, and Harold, to, uh, to not need attention from other people but just need Your love and attention. And please keep Kayla from telling lies about my best friend! In Jesus Name, Amen."

Maggie couldn't think of anything else to pray so she just agreed, "Amen."

When she raised her head, she saw that some of the others had been watching them as they bowed their heads. *Well so what? I don't want to care what anyone thinks about me except You, Lord.*

Danny said, "I have a secret that's been bothering me. There's something about Harold that the others don't know. You know we weren't allowed to bring phones or ipads or anything like that, but Harold snuck his in and plays games on it all the time." Danny hesitated. "I've wondered if I should tell his Senior but telling on somebody goes against everything I believe in."

"I know," Maggie answered. "You are the biggest hero in my opinion the way you took the blame for those boys on the hay wagon instead of telling on them."

Danny blushed. And Maggie's heart warmed toward him.

Just then Amy went to the front and called them all to silence.

"I have an announcement . From what I understand there have been several of you who have asked about the rest of the buildings and places on the grounds of The Kingdom Project."

There were murmurs of excitement around the room.

Amy laughed and continued. "We are going to take some tours later today. The first will be on lunch break and the second at dinnertime and the rest of the evening."

Maggie looked over at Whitney's table and grinned at her roommate, who held up two thumbs.

Amy continued. "At noon we will take you by bus to the adult retreat center and to the King's Chapel. In between we will have lunch with the grown ups who are staying at the center. When the afternoon classes are over, we'll give you a 30 minute break so you can go to your cottages. Then we'll take you, again by bus, to The Kingdom Project office, where you will learn more about our purposes, and the King's Shoppe where you can see the Christian books, toys, jewelry, clothes and things we have there, and then on to the Castle for dinner."

A room full of applause interrupted anything else Amy was going to say. But she just smiled. "God bless you all!"

Chapter Thirteen

A Dream Come True

Maggie could hardly pay attention in the healing class because of daydreaming about the tours of what she knew now were The Kingdom Project grounds. But then she felt guilty. This class was why she was here, to learn more to help Celie.

She'd learned about forgiveness and Amy and Gary said that when you forgave, all the anger and bitterness left. So she must not have forgiven Kayla. *What a failure I am!*

Finally the class was over and Maggie pasted a smile on her face and headed for the bus. All the kids fit in one bus so Maggie slid in beside David, and that was a relief. He was always so sensible and calm.

"Are you okay, Mags?" he asked, in a low voice which was probably unnecessary because there was so much excited chatter going on.

"No, not really." She answered honestly. "I'm having a really hard time about Kayla. I heard her telling lies about me. And I want to forgive her but I still feel angry so I guess I haven't really. And David," she paused, wondering if it was okay to repeat what happened in their group. "I know you won't repeat this but we were talking the other night with Beth and Brian at the cottage and she just blew up and said Jesus wasn't real and if He was, He wouldn't heal…" She paused; she couldn't tell anybody else about Celie, she'd already broken her promise to her parents. "He wouldn't heal people. Then she and Beth went off to Kayla's room and when Beth came out she told us Kayla wouldn't be out again. Obviously she's hurting about something and I should feel sorry for her. But all I can think is that I wish I'd never mentioned this camp to her. She's totally ruined my time here." And then she took a deep breath.

David looked at her with sympathetic eyes. "Maggie, I'm sure the Lord had you do that and by the end of camp, Kayla will be a new creature in Christ."

If David thought so, it must be true. This time Maggie breathed a sigh of relief. And nodded. "Okay. I will believe that too." She grinned. "Because I trust you."

"Uh Oh." David grinned back. "Now you're trying to make me proud."

Just then the bus came to a halt. The Retreat Center had cottages like the Fun To Be One Club Camp but they weren't as fun looking, just normal, and there were some larger and smaller.

Beth got up and began telling them about the center. "Sometimes a person may want to have a retreat by themselves and that's why there are little cottages. Sometimes there are groups like yours so there are some four bedroom cottages but with only two single beds in each bedroom. Grownups don't like bunk beds much." The kids laughed.

"And the building that is larger like where you checked in and eat your meals is just like yours." Then she answered

Maggie's unasked question. "Even to the shining knight armor! But that's not where we will be having lunch. The adults staying in the cottages helped our staff in preparing your picnic lunch in the area behind the center. And they are waiting for you now." She turned to the seniors, both guys and girls. "Seniors, gather your groups and take them around to the picnic area."

Sarabeth's group was one of the first to go around the building. Maggie and Whit both stopped abruptly at the sight that greeted them. It was like an enchanted forest with a blue stream running through it. They had seen the tops of trees over the roofs but never dreamed of the beauty beneath. There was a long patio beside the stream with pots of flowers spaced evenly and picnic tables between the flowers. There were two tables for each cottage of kids. And on the table were boxes, each with a name printed on it. Maggie found hers and walked over to stand behind the bench where the box was sitting on the table. She was glad to see Whit's next to hers and Kayla's at another table.

Maggie was really curious about what happened when Beth talked to Kayla alone in the bedroom but it obviously hadn't changed anything considering the girl's smirk in taking Danny's remark the wrong way when they were talking together at dinner the night before. She sighed, still feeling guilty about the fury that often rose up in her against her penpal. Oh how she wished she had never signed up for that.

"Hi kids!" She was surprised to see Abe, with his funny little hat. They hadn't seen him since the first night.

"We're so glad you came to join us for lunch. Isn't this beautiful?" He turned and waved his hand at the forest and stream. And all the kids clapped their hands.

Then he led them in a blessing over the food and after he said "Amen" all the kids eagerly opened their boxes. Maggie was surprised when she did; she was expecting sandwiches and chips but there were two chicken legs, an ear of corn on the cob, some cole slaw and one of those large, soft chocolate chip cookies. She saw that Whit had the same except her chicken was a breast. Then she remembered Sarabeth starting a talk one night about what kind of chicken each of the girls in her cottage liked. And they had all told her. That must be why the boxes had names on them. How neat! Then there were men and women bringing around trays of drinks - bottled water, colas, sweet tea - and they could choose what they wanted. Maggie and Whit both took a bottled water. "Thank you," Maggie said to the woman.

The lady smiled a big smile and said "You're welcome. Are you liking your stay at the Fun To Be One Club Camp?"

Uh oh! How do I answer that? Then it came to her how she could show appreciation without lying.

"This is the most fascinating place I've ever been. All three classes are wonderful and the meals are great. And I've made a wonderful new friend."

The woman beamed. "I'm so glad. What are you taking?"

Maggie smiled, "Biblical Healing, Drawing, and Horseback Riding."

The woman nodded. "Are you staying for next week?"

Maggie was quiet for a minute. "I'm not sure, but I have to decide today, don't I? See, my little sister is sick and I hate to leave her for two weeks. But..." she looked up at the lady. "I want to find out all I can about getting God to heal."

The woman was quiet for a minute. "What's your name?"

When Maggie told her, she replied. "I'm going to put Maggie and Maggie's sister on my prayer list tonight. I'll pray you have wisdom about staying at camp and that 'Maggie's sister" get healed. Is that okay?"

"Oh yes, thank you Ma'am. What is your name?"

"My name is Betsy. Oh, here comes Abe. I think he is going to share with you while you all eat. Glad to have met you, Maggie."

Maggie smiled at her. "I'm really glad to have met you too, Betsy."

Abe stood in the middle of the space between the patio and the stream. "I'm going to share a little bit with you about myself - and why I wear the hat that I do."

Maggie took her first bite of delicious fried chicken as he began.

"I have been fascinated with Israel all my life and when I got old enough I did some genealogy and found out that my grandmother on my mother's side was Jewish. That meant I am part Jewish. And I was really glad." He grinned at them. "I've been to Israel eleven times and I love it. Many Jewish men wear hats like these on their heads, mostly the Orthodox Jews who follow the law and always cover their heads. Others wear them sometimes when they go to prayer or a religious event. I wear them because I am proud to be a physical descendent of Abraham even though I am mostly a Christian."

Maggie nodded and noticed that Danny and David were nodding too.

"Do any of you have any questions about Israel or the Jews?"

Maggie was horrified when she saw Kayla raise her hand. Abe pointed to her.

"Is it true that all Jews are interested in is making money?"

Abe chuckled. "Jews are usually very wise about money and successful in business because they are raised to be responsible and to tithe. But it's just a myth that they are mostly greedy. I was never good at having money. I mostly give it away." He laughed again. "But I'm mostly a Christian." Then he sobered. "Unfortunately, Jews are often hated, slandered and persecuted and have been since their existence. Because they are God's chosen people and the devil hates that."

Kayla spoke up again without raising her hand. "Why are they chosen more than any of the rest of us?" She said it very sarcastically. Maggie slid down in her chair, ashamed again that she had told her penpal about the camp.

But she didn't seem to bother Abe a bit. "They were chosen because they listened to Yahweh, God. Abraham is one of the first, along with Enoch and Moses. He was raised in a pagan land but obeyed God to even go to a land that he didn't know about. I really respect him. That's why my name is now Abe. I changed it from Larry. In fact it was Amy who told me many years ago that the Lord told her that He was changing my name to Abraham. Then there's Moses, who was living a princely life, left all the luxuries behind to save his birth people, the Jews, and ended up receiving the Ten Commandments." He grinned. "But we learn that, because of what Yeshua, or Jesus, did, we Christians are now part of God's chosen people. Isn't that great?"

Maggie sneaked a glance toward Kayla and saw she was frowning. Maggie didn't hear much of the rest of the session because she was distracted by her own thoughts.

When lunch was over, they walked over to the King's Chapel. It was beautiful with lovely stained glass windows. Every other one had a golden cross surrounded by colors and in between each was a golden crown surrounded by colors. Then there were gorgeous crystal chandeliers and each pew had what looked like a large pearl at the end by the pathway in the middle of the chapel. At the front of the chapel was a lovely picture of a sea that covered the whole back wall of the chapel. There was a baptismal pool in front of it.

Maggie saw that there were communion things on the table below the pool - a tray with what looked like french bread and a goblet that she was sure was filled with grape juice. And some other things on the other side of the table.

Then Gary and Brian stood up and Gary welcomed them. "Welcome to the King's Chapel. This is where we gather sometimes for praise and worship and sometimes for Holy Communion. Today that is our mission." He held up the bread and said, "This represents the Body of Christ" he broke the bread in half, "which was broken for us." He set the bread back down and picked up the goblet. "This represents the Blood of Jesus which was shed for us, to wash away our sins and give us His life and nature." He smiled. We use grape juice instead of wine. I know some of you are used to communion wafers and individual cups and we have that for those who prefer."

When he said that, Brian picked up a round tray filled with small cups that were filled with the grape juice and a tray of small pieces of what looked like crackers. Then he spoke. "One of the really neat things about this kind of wafers is that they are unleavened bread which is what Jesus used at the Last Supper, where He and the disciples celebrated together. Leaven represented sin and the Jews cleared their homes of all leaven during that time. Notice that it's pierced and has stripes on it. Does that remind you of anything? Most of the kids were nodding. "Yes, this bread also represents Jesus and what He suffered."

Then Gary spoke again. "That is a wonderful way to celebrate what Jesus offers us - His body and blood. But this other way is wonderful too. It's called taking communion by Intinction. Each person pulls off a piece of the bread and dips it into the cup. This represents that you are part of the Body of Christ dipping yourself in His blood to be cleansed from sin and be like Him. You can choose today whichever way you want to partake. Some places have rules that you have to have been baptized or even belong to their church before you can partake.

But here at the King's Chapel we believe this truly is the Lord's Supper and He invites all to come. There have even been times when people received Jesus as their Savior for the first time while doing this."

Brian spoke again. "So you choose which way feels right to you. Marie is going to play and sing the hymn "Just As I Am" as you come, starting with the back row. And you can come down the center aisle to either place and then go back to your seats down the aisles beneath the windows."

Maggie looked back and saw the Seniors guiding each row as to when they were to step out in the aisle. Since Kayla was seated at the other end of the pew behind Maggie, she watched to see if the girl went forward. And prayed *Please Lord, let this be Kayla's time. You have invited her to Yourself, to give her new life. Help her… help her accept your invitation and be one of those who accepts you as her Savior during this time.* She was surprised to see both Kyliegh and Mary Katherine move toward the left and into the bread dipping line. And several she knew that were used to dipping the bread went to the cracker type line. Then to her shock she saw Kayla go up and get in the cracker type line, take the unleaven bread and then empty a cup. Then the girl whispered something to Brian and it held up the line but for some reason it didn't irritate Maggie. Brian nodded and pointed to the other line and Kayla went to it.

Then Maggie realized Susie was signaling her to step into the aisle. She stepped out and bent her head around the person in front of her and saw Kayla whisper to Gary and then partake of the dip the bread part. When Kayla went to the left aisle and back toward her seat, Maggie was really in shock because she saw tears streaming down Kaylas's face. *I shouldn't be shocked, Lord. I prayed for this. Thank you!"*

She decided to stick to her own way of doing Communion and got in Gary's line. Though she really liked the idea of the unleaven bread with piercings and stripes, both ways were filled with deep meaning. She couldn't help but love the "Fun to Be One" idea that each one tearing off the one piece of bread represented.

When all were back in their seats, Marie asked them to join her in singing "Just As I Am" and told them the music was in a place on the back of the pew in front of them. They all sang together and then the Seniors walked to the front and started guiding the rows down the center aisle and back to the bus.

Chapter Fourteen

Delight Abounds

That afternoon with Deuce was wonderful. Maggie decided it was because she wasn't stressed that he was calm and loving again. Patty let them ride most of the time. They rode around the paddock and then she and her personal horse, Thunderman, led them out of the paddock and through a trail in the woods. Maggie thought that was the best time she'd ever had in her life. Then she felt guilty because she should have enjoyed the King's Chapel more. But she mumbled aloud, "Accuser of the brethren, go away. God paired me up with Deuce so I am supposed to be having the best time in my life. So there!" And she enjoyed the rest of the classtime. She just had to stay next week or this would be her last time with Deuce. That shouldn't be her reason; it should be learning more about healing for Celie. *But it can be both, can't it Lord?*

On the way home, Danny sat with her instead of his new friends. He whispered, "Did you see Kayla go up for communion?"

Maggie nodded. "Both kinds! I'd love to know what she

said to Brian and Gary."

"Me too!" Danny answered. "I wonder if we'll ever find out."

Maggie shrugged. "Oh, I've decided to stay next week. I want to learn more." She grinned. "And be with Deuce more. And I feel like I wasted all these days being upset over Kayla. I'm not going to do that anymore!"

"Did she say anything when the bus took you back to your cottage?"

Maggie shook her head. "No, she went to her room and I didn't see her again before I left for class. I'm always the first to leave after lunch because we're the furthest away and this hay wagon comes before the bus. But we'll see her when we go to the King's Shoppe and the castle in a little while. Well, I guess I'll see her at the cottage for our half hour before we leave on the bus." She shrugged. "But she still might not be speaking to me."

"Let me know if you find out anything," Danny said.

"Of course I will."

When Maggie got back to the cottage, she immediately went in to her room and washed her hands and face and changed clothes. Her roommates were there too but they didn't have to change clothes because their afternoon activities hadn't been as physically challenging as hers. When there were about fifteen minutes left 'til the bus was due, there was a knock on their door. When Maggie opened it, Kayla was standing there, with a very unKayla-like look on her face.

"Can I talk to you, Maggie? Outside on the porch, in the rocking chairs?"

Maggie nodded and followed her penpal out the front door of the cottage. When they were both settled in the wooden rockers, Kayla began.

"I want to apologize for the way I've acted, Maggie." Tears welled up in the girl's eyes. "To everybody, but especially to you. Today during the time at the adults retreat center I felt bad because I was being disrespectful to Abe but he was so kind to me anyway. And then when we got to the King's Chapel and Brian was talking about the stripes and piercings on the Bread and how it was… unleavened I think he said… I felt something I never felt before. It was like Jesus was there with me, whispering, "I was without sin and did that for you, Kayla. I was beaten, had awful stripes on my back and I was pierced, nailed to the cross. All for you. And I did it for your baby brother who is with me now." Then Kayla started crying, her shoulders heaving and sobs coming from her mouth.

Maggie got up and went to the other rocker and put her arms around Kayla. "I didn't know you had lost a baby brother, Kayla. I'm so sorry. But I'm glad you heard Jesus."

Kayla got control of herself. "That's why I stopped believing in Jesus. We prayed and prayed. He was a year old when we found out he had Leukemia. But prayer didn't work and he died when he was a year and a half. I was eight years old then and my parents stopped going to church and they started fighting a lot. And you know what's going on now. I just thought there couldn't be a God." Then she smiled a weak smile. "But now I know there is. He talked to me."

At the word Leukemia Maggie got nauseated but she reminded herself that this time was not about her or her family but about Kayla. She hugged her and went back to her own rocking chair. "Now I understand. And I have to ask your forgiveness, Kayla. I thought you were awful." She paused and then went on. "I heard you tell lies about me. I was coming to the bathroom and heard you saying I was boy crazy and chase boys. And that's just not true. I have good friends who are boys but I don't think of them as anything but friends. Anyway, after that I was really angry. I hated you and I knew that was a sin. But finally today I prayed you would find Jesus."

Kayla's smile grew stronger. "See! And your prayer worked. And I'm sorry about the lies. I was saying you were what I am...I mean was. I'm not going to be that anymore. After we got back they let me skip the afternoon class and I talked with Amy and Gary and accepted Jesus as my Savior." Her eyes lit up. "And they called my parents and they said yes, I can be baptized in the King's Chapel."

"Oh, Kayla, I'm so glad. So happy for you. You get to be baptized in the very place that you first heard the Lord!"

Just then the bus honked and pulled up to the cottage.

"But don't tell anybody else yet, Maggie. They have a plan."

"Okay."

The other girls in the cottage, especially Whitney, looked surprised when Maggie and Kayla were the first on the bus. And chose to sit together.

Chapter Fifteen

Uh Oh and Oh Wow

The bus took them first to the gate way at the front and then straight back toward the Kingdom Project building. It was just a regular office building, nothing fancy, two floors of offices, but on the first floor one half of the building's main floor was a conference room, and they were guided into that. Amy and Gary were standing on a small platform with Beth and Brian sitting on chairs behind them. When they were all seated, Amy went to a podium.

"Welcome to the Kingdom Project central offices. I wanted to be the one to tell you about it" her eyes twinkled, "because it was my idea. I know the Lord gave it to me because it has come to pass. But it was over forty years after I saw the vision. I knew the Lord wants us - His Body in the earth - to be one. The first thing I started was a local Fun To Be One Club where people from all backgrounds and races and ages came together once a month for dinner, fun, and worship. It lasted several years. I started study groups, retreats, and conferences that in-cluded anyone. But I always saw that the Kingdom Project should be something that reached out to all communities with the "Fun To Be One Club" concept. And I saw this center - offices to oversee all the outreaches, The King's Shoppe to provide Christian toys, clothing, household items, books and other things. Back then you didn't see Christian merchandise, but of course there are many of those things available in many stores now. I saw retreat centers, one for adults and one for kids. I saw the King's Chapel. And another desire of my heart, The King's Castle, which you will see in a little while and have dinner there. We are so glad you are here. Already many wonderful things have been done by the King - and you will hear about these later. Now there is just this conference room and offices here so I'm sure you'd rather go straight on to the King's Shoppe. If there is an item you want, tell the people at the desk your name. Unknown to you, your parents sent money to an account for you to purchase things from the shop. Have fun and I'll see you at the castle!"

The King's Shoppe was right next door so they all just walked over.

It really was amazing. As soon as they stepped inside, they all seemed to separate and go to the sections that most grabbed their interest - jewelry, books, sports equipment, toys, clothes. And everything had a crown and a cross on it somewhere in different designs.

As Maggie walked through the jewelry section on her way to the books, she saw a necklace with a golden cross that had, instead of a sign at the top, a golden crown. She'd never been in to jewelry but she loved it. When she looked at the price, she wondered if her parents had put enough money into her account. She turned around and went to the desk. She immediately recognized Betsy from lunchtime.

Betsy remembered her too. "Hi Maggie. Glad to see you again." She turned to the lady beside her. "Christy, this is

Maggie. Maggie, Christy, we are cousins."

Maggie smiled. "That is neat! I wish I had a cousin. I just wondered, are we able to find out how much our parents put on our...our accounts or whatever it's called. There's a necklace over there I saw and really liked. It's a cross with a crown on top."

Betsy nodded. "That's a very popular one. I can't tell you how much they put in but I can tell you if you have enough to buy it. What is your last name?"

"Kelly."

Betsy looked through some papers and then looked up and smiled. "Oh yes, you have enough for that and a few other things too."

"Thank you." And she turned back to the shop to look for something for her twin sisters.

She had definitely decided not to leave the next day but when she did leave, she would take them both a present. After looking at the toys and the clothes, she went back to the desk.

"Betsy, do I have enough to get three of those necklaces? I have two sisters, not just one. They are twins."

Betsy nodded. "Yes you do, Maggie. Why don't you go get three now before someone else buys them."

So she did. And after she had them wrapped in tissue and in a sack and after she had thanked Betsy, she saw Ray and Danny over in the corner whispering to each other.

Joining them she asked, "What's going on, guys?"

Ray looked at Danny who nodded. "I saw Harold slip a keychain into his pocket. Then he went up and got a tee shirt and a football and took them to the desk."

Maggie clenched her teeth. "What happened to him? I thought he was a Christian now."

Ray looked sad. "But all Christians are not perfect. Well none of us. But stealing is really bad. What should we do?"

"I can't tell on him. I just can't" Danny said.

Maggie hung her head. "I don't want to."

Ray said, "Maybe we should tell him we know?"

Danny shrugged and Maggie said, "You two can do it, I can't."

"But you can pray, right?" Danny asked.

"Yes, I can pray. And I will."

Just then they saw the lady who had been at the desk beside Betsy walk over to Harold.

"That's Christy," said Danny. "She's really nice. Patrick, my Senior, said she teaches some of the classes sometimes."

"She's Betsy's cousin." Maggie added.

Within a minute Christy and Harold had walked out the door. The three looked at each other and then went to the front window of the shop. They saw Harold reach in his pocket and hand the keychain over to the lady, but he kept his head bowed and didn't look up at her. She patted him on the shoulder and said something and then headed toward the door. The three of them then scattered to different parts of the shop.

Soon the bus pulled up in front of The King's Shoppe. The Seniors gathered their groups and they all got on the bus again.

The bus took them through some trees and then through a thicker bunch of trees, almost like a forest again. And then they came to a clearing. Several gasps were heard throughout the bus. There was a long driveway with old fashioned light posts on each side and the driveway led to a castle. It really did remind Maggie of Cinderella's castle at DisneyWorld. *Wow!*

When they got out of the bus, nobody was talking. Even though the sky was still bright, the gas lights were on. They walked through the tall carved double doors and were greeted by a man with very white hair. He was dressed in a suit and wore a smile.

"Hello, my name is King David and I'm happy to welcome

you to the King's Castle."

Well that's weird.

"As you can see, it's a very special place." And he waved his hands at all the tapestries on the walls that surrounded them. Walls at least sixty feet tall. To his right was a marble staircase and Maggie wondered what was upstairs, almost as much as she wondered why he called himself a king.

The man continued, "Just go through the doors there to your left and you'll find your banquet tables. They have place cards, so look for your own names. And don't be surprised when you see 'King' in front of your name. Just remember that you are a royal priesthood, kings under the King of Kings. And in the King's Castle, we never forget that."

Maggie thought '*Oh, now I get it!*'

They filed silently into the large dining hall which was as beautiful as the entrance hall and the stairway. In the center of each table was a flower arrangement around a lit candle. And the plates were a beautiful amber with gold specks on them. Maggie finally found the King Maggie Kelly name tag and was pleased to see that she was seated between Whitney and David. She couldn't see the name part of the place card across from her but was even more pleased when Danny sat down there. Ray sat next to him but the rest of their group... no, Polly sat on the other side of Whitney. The others were pretty far away.

Whitney leaned over and giggled as she said, "King Whitney really sounds weird."

"No more than King Maggie but if the Bible said that's who we are I guess it's who we are."

King David went to the front of the room and began talking. "I have a few announcements to make before our dinner. When we leave here we will have a bonfire and roast marshmallows." In any other place, there would have been clapping, but Maggie guessed the others were feeling as awed as she was about their surroundings.

He continued. "We will have some baptisms at the King's Chapel tomorrow right after lunch. And as you probably know, some will be leaving in the afternoon, and others will be joining us for next week."

Then King David led them in a prayer to bless their meal. After that he sat down and Beth and Brian, Amy and Gary, Abe, Betsy, Christy, and several other staff came out pushing carts filled with food which they passed around. There was turkey and roast beef, mashed potatoes, two kinds of gravy, green beans, peas, creamed corn, tossed salad with the dressing of your choice, and rolls. They each served themselves and took as much as they wanted. The server at Maggie's table was named King Daniel and he told them that dessert choices would be out after they finished their dinner. Those choices would be chocolate cake with whipped cream, bread pudding with caramel sauce, or lemon pie.

When he had rolled the cart away, Maggie looked around at her friends. "We really are being treated like royalty!" They all agreed.

Chapter Sixteen

Faith and Fun

They all left the castle, very full, and very quiet. All they had done was eat. There were no more prayers or talks of any kind. When everyone was full, the Seniors gathered their groups and headed out to the bus.

Kayla walked up to Maggie and said, "Can we sit together again?" Maggie had wanted to sit with Danny and talk about the incident with Harold at the King's Shoppe, but Kayla looked so unsure of herself that she put on a big smile and grabbed Kayla's hand. "Sure."

When they were seated, Kayla said, "That was something, wasn't it? I admit I don't understand what that King stuff was all about?"

Maggie laughed. "It surprised me. But I think it meant that we are now, inside at least, like God created Adam and Eve to be. Having authority in the earth. And that man, King David, quoted some scripture from the Bible about us being a royal priesthood and a holy nation. In another place in the Bible, Jesus is called the King of Kings. And that means He is the King over us who are now royal because we have been born again and are now His Body in the earth."

Kayla frowned. "I have a lot to learn. I don't even understand all of what you just explained to me."

Maggie laughed. "Neither do I, Kayla. Neither do I!"

Just then the bus pulled up at the adult retreat center again and the Seniors led them around to where they had eaten lunch.

It was getting dark now so they didn't quite have the beautiful scene that greeted them at noon, but there was a fire built in the center of the yard and jars with thin wooden sticks on them sitting on a table. On another table were bowls of marshmallows.

The two girls grinned at each other. Then Kayla surprised her.

"I'm going to go sit with those girls I was with most of the week. I want to tell them I lied about you, Maggie." She looked a little scared. "Will you pray for me."

Maggie reached over and hugged her and whispered, "Lord help Kayla know she is forgiven by You and by me. And give her just the right words to say to her friends so they will still be friends with her. In Jesus Name, Amen."

"Thank you!" Kayla returned the hug before she left to join the other group.

Maggie looked around and Danny immediately joined her. "That's quite a miracle, Maggie. I mean you and Kayla."

"I know. Jesus has really worked a miracle in her." Then she laughed. "So I've forgiven God for having me telling her about the Fun To Be One Club Camp."

He laughed too. Then Harold came up to them. A lot of the other kids were already picking up marshmallows and putting them on the end of sticks. But he said "Can I talk to you guys?"

"Sure." Danny answered. They all sat down on the ground away from the rest of the others.

"I want to confess something." He looked uncomfortable. "Today I stole something from the King's Shoppe." Then he grinned, sort of. It was more of a grimace. "Well, I tried to steal something. But I got caught. See, my parents told me about putting money on that account and told me how much. It was enough to cover two things I wanted. But I wanted three. So I took the third, a keychain, and put it in my pocket." He shook his head. "How dumb is that? Stealing a keychain because it has a cross and crown on it? Anyway, one of the women saw me and had me give it back. I told her I was sorry and asked if I could be baptized. I accepted Jesus as my Savior but was never baptized. They just told me on our way out of the castle that they called my parents and I can be baptized tomorrow."

"Oh Harold!" Maggie said. "That's wonderful."

Danny stuck out his hand. "Way to go, Brother!" The two slapped hands together.

Then Harold looked at them both solemnly. "Thank you both!!! I don't deserve your friendship but I sure am glad I have it."

"It's fun to be one, right?" Maggie grinned.

"Yes!" Both boys said at the same time.

Then they all three joined the marshmallow roasting crowd.

Maggie saw Danny go over and talk to Ray so she knew he was telling him about Harold's confession.

It had been a long day and an emotional one. Maggie was ready to go back to their cottage and go to sleep but the others seemed to be wide awake and having fun, as she yawned. Then Gretchen came over to her.

"Hi, Maggie. I feel like I never see you anymore. I miss you." Her slender eyes looked sad.

"I miss you too, Gretchen. It's been a rough week for me but I think everything is okay now."

"Was it that Kayla person?"

Maggie nodded. "But guess what? She accepted Jesus as her Savior during Holy Communion this morning and is going to be baptized tomorrow."

"Wow, that's great. Wonder who else? They said baptisms plural."

"Well, I don't know if there are any more but Harold hasn't been baptized since he accepted the Lord and he told Danny he is going to be baptized tomorrow!" She didn't want to tell Gretchen about Harold stealing things.

"Yes!" Gretchen pumped her hand with a thumbs up."

"I'm glad but to tell you the truth I'm too tired to be excited. I wish they'd let me go back and go to sleep."

"I hope you feel better soon." And Gretchen hugged her and left.

A few minutes later, Sarabeth came over and said, "I'm tired, Maggie, and ready to go back to the cottage. Susie said she'd make sure any of my cottage that wanted to stay would get back safely. Which would you want to do?"

Relief flooded Maggie. "Oh, go with you. Definitely!"

The bus delivered most of their cottage, and lots of other cottages too along with their Seniors. Whit came back but Kayla didn't. She really seemed to be enjoying herself. And Maggie was glad.

The next morning Kayla was so excited she hugged every girl in their cottage and told them how if it weren't for Maggie she would be going to hell instead of being baptized that morning,

Maggie just shook her head. "No way, Kayla. Jesus would have found some other way to reach you."

But Kayla just hugged her again.

Sarabeth surprised them by bringing in a white robe. "Try

this on, Kayla."

"What is it?"

"It's a baptismal robe. I think it's your size."

Kayla put it on over her clothes and it fit perfectly.

Maggie was surprised that there was a robe large enough for Kayla there in their cottage but she sure wasn't going to say anything. And she was a little jealous. When she was baptized, she just wore regular clothes but Kayla was going to get to wear something special. Then she shook herself. Jealous. How stupid. It didn't matter what anybody wore; what mattered was that they were giving their life to Jesus and asking Him to cleanse them from sin and give them the Holy Spirit.

After breakfast, it wasn't too long until the bus pulled up out front.

When they were at the King's Chapel, everyone poured out of the bus and several of the adults took Kayla, Harold, and two kids that Maggie didn't know through a door in the back.

The baptismal font seemed even more beautiful today since it was going to be used.

They all sat quietly as King David and King Gary each baptized two of the kids who wanted to be baptized. They were all asked the same questions and when they agreed, asked to repeat the same things.

"I believe that Jesus is the Christ, the Son of the living God. I believe He died for my sins and rose again to give me new life. I believe in the Holy Spirit who is given to me."

And then. "Jesus I receive new life from You." And , "Jesus I give You my life to use me as You will."

Then the baptizer said, "I baptize you in the name of the Father, Son, and Holy Spirit." And when they came up out of the water, "Lord bless this child of yours. Fill them with your Holy Spirit. Guide and direct all the days of his/her life. In Jesus Name, Amen."

The ceremony didn't last long and then the bus took them all to the castle again for a lunch. This time they could sit where they wanted and there were buffet tables against the walls so they could serve themselves. When they were all seated at the tables with their food, they knew to wait until some-one said the blessing. This time it was a new lady.

"Hi, my name is Ginny. I couldn't get here until this morning but I am going to say the blessing. This is a sad day for some who are leaving after one week, or who have friends who are leaving. But the Lord will be sending new friends and we know all of you who stay will do your best to make them feel at home. But remember, don't give away any of the secrets. Let them learn about the King's Chapel, the King's Shoppe, and the King's Castle, the way you did. Okay?" They all nodded at the pretty lady with auburn hair. And then she said the blessing.

When lunch was over, the bus took them back to their cottages so those who were leaving could begin to pack. Maggie was glad that everybody in her cottage was staying for the second week. Sarabeth and Whitney, Christy, Tori, Midge, Marge, Carolyn, Linda, Sandy, Lyla, and even Kayla all seemed like family now.

Sarabeth said, before they could get to their rooms, "We'll be on the bus again in an hour to go to the Kingdom Project Offices to say goodbye to those who are leaving. Then the newcomers will be coming about an hour after that. But" and she smiled around at everybody, "we won't have any coming to our cottage because we aren't losing anyone."

Most of the girls went to their rooms to read or take a nap but Maggie, Tori, and Lyla decided to get out a puzzle they found in one of the cabinets. It was of Pinocchio in a forest standing near a little cottage, with Jiminy Cricket on the roof. But there were a thousand pieces.

Tori said "Do you think we can finish this in a week?"

Lyla answered, "Sure! Can't we Maggie?"

Maggie looked at all the little pieces. "But where can we do it? We use the table for meals sometimes." Then she knocked on Sarabeth's door. When the Senior answered, Maggie asked. "Where can we work a puzzle?" And she pointed to the box on the table.

Sarabeth turned and in a minute brought out a card table. "This is here mostly for puzzles! You can leave it out until we leave." She grinned."Just don't put it in front of a door."

"Great," Maggie said and took the card table. Within five minutes, the girls had begun looking for edge pieces. Within thirty minutes they had one side edge put together.

But soon it was time for goodbye's and they all filed out to the bus when it pulled up.

It was sad. Some of the girls who were going home were crying and hanging on to their Seniors or cottage mates. The boys looked sad and like they didn't want to go either.

"Can't they stay if they've changed their minds?" Maggie asked Sarabeth. She shook her head. "No, there are others on the way to take their places. And most of them have family vacations or other commitments. They'll be okay." She patted Maggie on the shoulder.

After the one-week-only kids and their families had gone, everyone who was left returned to their cottages. They didn't have anything left to do until supper. Some of the other cottages would be welcoming their new friends but the inhabitants of Peace Cottage had leisure to do whatever they wanted. Maggie, Tori, and Layla chose to go back to work on their Pinocchio puzzle.

Chapter Seventeen

Racism and Resolution

The weekend was not a fun time for Maggie. All she could think about was her baby sisters' bone marrow test on Monday. She believed she had never prayed so hard about anything, mostly that God would help Celie not feel pain and that the test would show she doesn't have cancer. She wanted to be there to hold her hand, to hug her, to tell her how much she is loved.

"How prideful I am! Her parents and twin can do all that." But then she thought, "But she said she misses me when I am gone."

Finally Sunday afternoon, during quiet time, she asked Sarabeth if she could talk to her.

"Sure." The Senior led Maggie out to a bench in the back yard of the cottage.

It was so pretty back there. There were pretty trees and several gardens, one filled with knock-out rose bushes, and the others with a combination of lilies, asters, hydrangea, some she didn't know, and Maggie's favorite - purple Hibiscus growing up on a white thing at the back of one of the gardens. It all reminded her of some pictures she'd seen of English gardens and she loved it.

As soon as they sat down, Sarabeth said, "Tomorrow's your sisters test, isn't it?"

Maggie's eyes filled with tears and she nodded. Her throat was so tight, she wasn't sure she could talk.

Sarabeth seemed to sense that. "Maggie, this must be hard for you, being here and away from her at a time like this." Maggie just nodded.

"I asked and found out that they should know the results of the test by Wednesday or Thursday. I hope you don't mind..." She grinned and then pulled Maggie into her arms. "I called your parents and they are going to call my cell phone as soon as they hear the results and either you can talk to them if we are together or if you're in class, I'll tell you as soon as class is over." Then she added, "We're not supposed to do this but I got permission from Amy since this is a special thing."

Maggie pulled herself away and looked at Sarabeth in awe, right before she burst into tears. Then she hugged her Senior again and got out two words. "Thank you!"

Something inside relaxed and she prayed silently, "Please Lord, let me not be in class when the call comes."

Monday morning Maggie got her cottage mates to pray that her sister's test would be easy on her and she wouldn't be afraid or hurt.

Kayla said, "I'll pray all day, I promise." Maggie remembered that her new friend had lost a little brother and she reached over and squeezed her hand.

Sarabeth had the others start out and she closed the prayer.

Maggie had signed up for the Walking by Faith class for the second week. She was pleased to find out that the new lady Ginny was teaching it. So after breakfast she hurried to the classroom and was the first one there.

Ginny was taking some papers out of a bag that had Disney princesses on it. That made Maggie smile. When Ginny looked up at her, Maggie said "I love Disney princesses."

"Which is your favorite?"

"I'm not sure. Maybe Belle, because she loved to read and so do I. Most of the kids like all the new ones. Mostly Elsa. But Anna is my favorite in that story. She's the hero. Well, I guess it's heroine."

Ginny grinned. "I'm with you."

"Who is your favorite princess?"

"Well, I'm kind of old fashioned. I like Cinderella best."

"Oh, me too, really. She was so real; she cried and got angry but she was still nice and hopeful."

Ginny nodded. "That's great…what's your name?"

"Maggie."

"Well Maggie, you've already got part of today's lesson."

Others started coming in to the class, some Maggie recognized and some she didn't. Ray was in this class and looked really glad to see her. He came to sit beside her. Harold was there too and sat on the other side of Ray. Then Polly came and sat right behind them on the second row. That made four of them from their own Fun To Be One Club. Even though the others didn't know about Celie, Maggie felt comforted by their presence.

When Ginny had finished checking the list and announced that they were all there, she had them go around and share their names. When a boy named Pete told his name, Ray hit Maggie's arm lightly with his elbow. When she looked over at him, he rolled his eyes. Then he wrote on a notebook page, "Tell you later."

Ginny began the class by reading the verse, "**Now faith is the substance of things hoped for, the evidence of things not**

seen." Hebrews 11:1. When she put her Bible down, she prayed, "Lord, help us truly understand what faith is, and how to live in it." Then she smiled at the whole class.

"You may have noticed my bag," and she held up the princess bag. "I know you guys are probably thinking 'Yuck' but I promise this whole class is not going to be girly. Okay?"

Several of the boys nodded, including Ray and Harold.

"Maggie and I were talking about princesses right before the rest of you got here. I said my favorite was Cinderella because she was real. She was treated badly and sometimes she cried and sometimes she got mad. But on the whole, she was pleasant to people, found joy in the good things around her, and most of all as Maggie pointed out - she had hope.

"Our subject this week is faith. As I read, faith is the substance of things hoped for, the evidence of things not seen. Okay that's great, but where do you get this thing, faith, that makes all you hope for happen? Does anybody know?"

Several people raised their hands, including all her friends. Maggie thought she knew but wasn't sure.

"Well," Ginny continued, "For that verse to really make sense, you have to know another one. In Romans 10:17, we read '*So then faith comes by hearing and hearing by the Word of God.*' In other words, you get faith by hearing what God has to say about something and if He promises something that you hope for, and you believe Him, you will have what you believe and hope for. Does that make sense?"

Maggie looked back and everybody was nodding their heads.

"Cinderella's dreams came true. The movie doesn't mention God. But in the most recent one, not the cartoon but the one with real people, the last words Cinderella says as she looks back at her stepmother who has abused her so much, are, 'I forgive you.'

"I love that because it makes me think of another scripture, one that Jesus Himself said. I'll read more of it later in the week as we go deeper into understanding the workings of faith but this one is so very important that I want us to start off understanding that this is an important part of faith. In Mark 11:25, Jesus said, *"**And when you stand praying, forgive if you have anything against anybody, so that your Father in heaven may forgive your sins."***

Wow, every class I take teaches about forgiveness, Maggie thought.

Polly raised her hand, "Does that mean that if you don't ask God to forgive your sins, your prayers won't be answered?"

"That's a tough one, Polly." Ginny smiled. "There are people who are still sinning who get answered prayer. And it's really talking about forgiving others. But Jesus said this Himself, so," she shrugged, "I think to be sure, we should always forgive others. And I think that we should always ask that our own sins be forgiven."

There was more discussion. But mostly Maggie was glad she had forgiven Kayla and asked forgiveness for herself. She could feel hope about Celie rising up in her chest. Maybe the words Whitney heard really were from Jesus *It will be okay. I have healed her and she will be fine.* She wanted to believe that so much!

Lunch was good that day, hamburgers and french fries, tossed salad and both orange and chocolate cake. But the best was when Sarabeth came to Maggie's table and bent over to whisper in her ear. Your Mom went ahead and called me to tell you the test is over and Celie is fine and she said afterwards, "I could almost feel Maggie praying for me." Maggie couldn't keep from smiling. "Thank you, Sarabeth. So much."

That afternoon the time with Deuce was even better. Her afternoon class was the same as last week. Danny was taking something else, archery she thought, but she was determined to spend all the time with Deuce that she could.

It was between supper and the program that night that Ray finally got to talk to them about Pete. She, Harold, Danny and Polly were all seated with him outside the Clubhouse on some tree stumps put there for that purpose.

"I need you guys to tell me what to do. I've never had this happen before. That guy Pete just came in Saturday and when Jack brought him to my room, he pointed to me and said 'I'm not going to sleep in a room with that...' and he called me a name - the n word."

Maggie felt fury rising up inside her. "What did Jack do?"

Ray kind of grinned. "Well he said 'Ray, I'm sorry. I won't let you be exposed to this anymore.' Then he took Pete to another room." He paused. "In a little while one of the guys who was there last week brought his stuff to my room and took the vacant bed. He didn't say anything so I guess he knew why he was moved but I'm not sure."

Maggie said, the fury showing in her voice, "Why didn't they send him home? I'd like to...well I'm not sure what I'd like to do."

Harold spoke up. "It looks like you need to do some forgiving, Maggie." He grinned and then he turned to Ray with a more serious expression. "Have you forgiven him?" Then to Danny, "We learned about the importance of forgiveness in our class this morning."

Ray said, "Yes, I think so. I don't want him punished." And he grinned at Maggie. "But I do want him to change."

Danny said "I think we all do."

Ray said, "It reminds me of the Kingdom Tale about the wars."

Maggie nodded. "Yes, but that's what the Fun To Be One Club is all about. We're all one family in Jesus, whatever race or denomination. Why is that Pete person here if he thinks that way?"

"Maybe he doesn't understand," said Ray. "Maybe God sent him here for that reason."

"He probably wouldn't like me either," said Polly, her eyes narrowing.

"Anyway," Ray said, "I don't know what to do. Should I say something to him? Try to make friends?"

Harold shook his head. "I don't think so." Then he paused. "But you guys have been Christians longer than I have. What do you think?"

After a moment of silence, Maggie said, "I think you are right. Only Jesus can change people. I think maybe you could just smile at him when you see him, show him you aren't mad at him."

Ray grinned. "Well, I still am kind of mad. But I have forgiven him. So I'll smile. I'll probably be gritting my teeth at the same time."

They all laughed.

The next two days, Maggie watched at class and meal times; she saw Ray smile at Pete but it didn't look like Pete saw the smiles because he never looked at Ray. She surprised herself by not being anxious about the phone call from her parents about Celie. The Word of God said Jesus bore Celie's sicknesses and diseases and by Jesus stripes she is healed. *And I am hoping and believing that His Word will come true!*

It was Wednesday at lunch when Sarabeth motioned her to come outside the Clubhouse. She had a big grin on her face and Maggie's heart started beating fast.

Her hands were trembling when she took the phone from Sarabeth.

"Hi, Sweetheart. I have somebody that wants to talk to

you." In less than a second, Celie's voice announced, "I don't have any of those awful things, Maggie. The tests came out good."

"Thank you, God!" Maggie answered.

"Oh Mom says I have to get off. I love you."

"I love you, Celie, and I'm so happy."

Then her mother was back. "Maggie, they ruled out leukemia, meningitis, hepatitis, and cystic fibrosis. Do you remember when Celie had pneumonia and other congestion things last winter?" She didn't wait for Maggie's answer. "Well they now think it's something called Post Viral Syndrome. The Doctor said she needs lots of rest and a high protein diet and she should be fine in a month or two."

"Praise the Lord!" Maggie said.

"Praise the Lord indeed. Are you okay?"

"Yes! Even better now. I love camp."

"Good! I'm glad. See you Saturday! Have a wonderful rest of the week. I love you!"

"Love you too, Mom."

She handed the cell phone back to Sarabeth and they hugged and laughed with joy.

The kids looked at them a little strangely when they re-entered the dining room but they just ignored it. They would tell those in their cottage who knew about Celie later on.

Ray told them nothing had changed with Pete. He still never looked at Ray which was uncomfortable sometimes, especially in their cottage meetings and discussions. But then Friday came. They went to the King's Chapel for Holy Communion. Kayla sat beside Maggie and held her hand. It was the place where she was set free. And Maggie could feel the Presence of God there too.

It happened that when they lined up, Ray was right behind

Pete. Since the custom there was that each person put their hands on the shoulder of the person in front of them, Maggie wondered if Ray would move back. But he didn't. He put his hands on Pete's shoulder.

The other boy glanced back and looked surprised but not angry.

Now, Lord, please. Maggie prayed. *Do a miracle in Pete's heart. Ray has forgiven him and I forgive him. Please, You forgive him and put your love in his heart.*

Then they told Maggie's pew to get in line and she couldn't see any more.

She didn't have to. After she had taken communion, she turned to go back to her seat and saw Pete and Ray hugging each other in the side aisle. *Thank You. Thank You. Thank You!*

The next morning was sad. Everyone would have to leave and go home. Maggie found out that a staff member would take Kayla to the airport and she would fly home. But there was a surprise for her - a letter from her mother was handed to her at the Clubhouse. She opened it and showed it to Maggie, with a big grin on her face.

"Dearest Kayla, When we got the request for your baptism, we realized how wrong we have acted the past few years. So we went to church yesterday and rededicated our lives to the Lord. We are really excited for when you get home and we can all begin our new lives together. Love, Mom."

Maggie and Kayla hugged and Maggie said, "We will continue to be penpals, won't we?"

"Of course! I've written down my full name and address, regular e-mail address and phone number. I have my own cell, got it for Christmas."

"I don't have one."

"Well then give me your home phone and I'll call you."

So Maggie wrote down all her information "Oh, are you on Facebook?"

Kayla nodded. " Are you?"

"Yes!"

Kayla smiled, "We'll become friends there too!"

Susie joined them and said "It's time to leave for the airport, Kayla."

Kayla nodded and turned to hug Maggie. "Thank you again. Look what you've done for me and my parents just by telling me about the Fun To Be One Club."

Maggie would never let her know how much she regretted it earlier. But now she was so grateful to the Lord for doing it. They waved goodbye and Kayla turned back and yelled, "Pray I can lose weight."

Maggie nodded.

Just then a car drove up with a pretty woman in it. Whit ran toward the car and reached through the window to hug the woman. She listened for a minute and then turned around looking completely joyful. She came running back to get her suitcase and bag.

"Guess what, Maggie? She kicked him out. Craig's gone and there's a restraining order so he can't come back. And we're going to move to a new place! Just Mom and me! Please come and meet her."

So Maggie went with her to the car and was introduced to Whit's mother. She waved as they drove off.

Then Mr. and Mrs. Sanders drove up in their van and it was time to go.

Maggie looked around and discovered that she didn't want to leave the place she came to unwillingly. There had been so many miracles take place. So much love. She knew she'd never be the same. And she was so glad they had their own small club. She knew their adventures would even be more powerful after this experience. And they would be registered officially with the national club.

There was one more person she just had to say good-bye to.

Sarabeth enfolded Maggie in her arms. "It really is Fun To Be One, isn't it?"

Stories from Kingdom Tales

Harmony, Rhythm and the Wonderful Tree

Once upon a time there were twin princesses born to a King and Queen who loved music very much. They named the older princess Harmony and the younger Rhythm.

As the princesses grew older, everyone could see that they were well named. Harmony was adaptable and made everyone around her very happy, no matter where she was, or who she was with, or what the circumstances were. Rhythm was very steady and practical and brought order wherever she went.

Harmony respected her twin for she could see that, even though she herself was always content, things in the kingdom were sometimes confusing and needed straightening up. It did seem to Harmony, though she didn't think about it a lot because she didn't want to be disloyal to her sister, that maybe dear Rhythm was a tiny bit harsh and rigid sometimes. There were people who didn't want to be straightened up and put in order quite as much as Rhythm insisted on.

Rhythm adored her older sister, though it seems strange to me, because Harmony didn't have a smidge of orderliness about her. But even though Rhythm couldn't stand disorder in anyone else, she thought Harmony was perfect just the way she was.

When it came time for the King and Queen to choose a successor to rule the kingdom, they considered the virtues of both of their daughters.

"Harmony was born first," said the Queen. "She should inherit the throne."

"But, my dear," the King said firmly, "Rhythm is so sensible and stable. The kingdom needs her good sense and organizational ability."

"I know," agreed the Queen. "But ..."

"But what?" demanded the King.

"Well, dear, Rhythm does tend to organize everyone to be exactly as she is herself. Think of the gardens."

The King saw immediately what the Queen meant.

The gardens were extremely important, for the economy of that kingdom was based on them. Each person had their own garden and produced what they grew best of fruit and vegetables and flowers. The King and Queen had often laughed secretly over the differences in their daughters' gardens.

Rhythm would not grow anything that could not be planted neatly - and kept that way! She grew very nice corn and broccoli and lettuces and tomatoes (on poles of course.) Her tulip bed was a picture of perfection and the grapes on her arbor were delicious and brought a great price in the Marketplace.

Harmony's garden was very different. She took care of it as well as her sister did hers, making sure that weeds were promptly dug out and everything watered properly. But it was not the neat, orderly place that Rhythm's garden was. Harmony insisted, "Let the dear things wander where they will. They know what's best for them." And we have to admit that her tomatoes really flourished, sprawling out wherever they wanted, and were the sweetest and juiciest in the kingdom. And the fragrance of her roses perfumed the entire Castle grounds.

The King pursed his lips and said, "If Rhythm were Queen, it would mean an end to melons."

"And strawberries," added the Queen.

"And squashes and several varieties of beans," the King agreed sadly.

"And wisteria and honey suckle and ... oh, a lot of lovely things," pleaded the Queen.

"But if Harmony is Queen, she won't insist on anything," argued the King. "She'll let everybody do just as they like and it may be that nobody grows peas or potatoes."

"Or asparagus or onions," agreed the Queen.

"It would probably be an end to orchids," added the King.

In the end, they decided that the two princesses would rule together with equal authority.

"They will balance each other," said the King, well pleased with their decision.

"And the kingdom will flourish," said the Queen happily.

This seemed like the perfect solution, and honestly I couldn't think of a better one myself. But when the time came that the King and Queen went across the sea to their retirement home, things did not go the way they had hoped.

When a plague of Woofle Worms attacked all the gardens of the kingdom, the sisters could not agree on what to do. Queen Harmony thought the natural defenses of the plants themselves and the insecticides with which the gardens were sprayed would take care of the problem. She refused to agree to any drastic measures to destroy "the poor little worms who are only doing what comes naturally."

But then word came pouring in from all corners of the

kingdom that almost half of the crops had been eaten. Finally Harmony said, "Do what you please!" And she ran crying to her room.

Queen Rhythm, in her determination to rid the kingdom of these new and different creatures, had such strong poisons sent to all the gardens that not only did all the Woofle Worms die, but so did the rest of the crops.

If the storehouses hadn't been stocked full during the years the King and Queen reigned, the kingdom would have been in real trouble that year. But as it was, there was plenty to carry them through.

There were other things that happened, but none as big and bad as the Woofle Worm disaster, so the sisters reigned in peace - mostly - for several years. And the kingdom got along fairly well.

One day word reached the Castle that a new variety of fruit tree was available at the Marketplace near the border. It was said that the flowers of that tree gave off the most wonderful scent imaginable and that poets and musicians exposed to that scent were inspired to create their greatest works. And when the fruit came in season - well, those who had eaten it swore it was the most delicious fruit ever, and that it even made them feel younger. The leaves of the tree were said to have a wonderful healing quality when brewed into a pleasant tasting tea.

When the sisters heard of this wonderful tree, they began a journey to the Marketplace to buy some seedlings for their kingdom. But halfway on their journey they were stopped by a landslide that blocked off the road ahead.

"We'll have to go back," said Rhythm.

"No! We must have those trees for the kingdom!" Harmony pointed to the left. "Look, there is a path in the woods. I'm sure we can find our way to the Marketplace through there."

But Rhythm would not try a new, unknown path. And

Harmony insisted on going on alone, no matter how much Rhythm told her how irresponsible it was, and how unfair to the people of the kingdom to take a chance that their ruler might be torn apart by wild beasts, or starve to death, or be lost forever in the forest.

Rhythm was so disgusted when she saw her obstinate sister square her shoulders and march off into the woods alone, that she returned to the Castle and removed all her own things. She took them to a palace at the east of the village that had been used as a summer vacation home by the royal family in earlier years.

When people asked her about this, she just said, "It's for the best." She still loved Harmony and would not say anything bad about her sister, but the truth was that she was very tired of the joint rule since they never saw things alike. And it never seemed right to her to have two rulers anyway, and after all, Harmony was the oldest. Besides she thought it was very stupid and selfish of her sister to go off alone on an unknown path which looked terribly wrong and dangerous. It make her frightened for Harmony and when someone is frightened, they don't think very clearly.

Meanwhile, Harmony had some difficulties on her journey through the woods. There were some uncomfortable times but Harmony adapted herself to the circumstances until she was safely through them. And she finally reached the Marketplace unharmed.

When she arrived back at the Castle with her wagonload of seedlings, Harmony was very sad to find that her sister had moved out. She sent many messages to the eastern palace begging Rhythm to return but the only reply she ever received was, "This is for the best."

It was so lonely in the Castle without Rhythm that after a few months, Harmony built another small palace on the western edge of the village and moved into it herself.

The great Castle stood empty and silent, and the citizens of the kingdom were not sure who their ruler was. Sometimes they would go to Rhythm for advice and sometimes to Harmony. And it happened that over the years most people would go first to one and then the other; and they would take bits and pieces of advice from each and come up with their own solutions. Actually this worked out very well, and in my opinion, should have been done all along, instead of the sisters thinking they had to come up with one perfect answer to everything.

And so the kingdom fared well even with the distance between the two Queens.

Harmony planted the seedlings near the western palace and after several years they grew to be a wonderful orchard with tall, strong trees. She never sent out announcements about the trees because she was afraid that Rhythm would think she was bragging about her successful journey. So, many people did not know of the wonderful new things available in their kingdom. But to those who asked, Harmony was very generous and gave them fruit and leaves, and new seedlings which she'd started herself.

It made Harmony sad when she thought of what an orchard of wonderful trees she and Rhythm together could have produced. And how Rhythm could have organized the transportation of the trees to all parts of the kingdom, and arranged exportation and trade with other kingdoms. But she tried not to think of those things which could have been but were not. And she spent her days in her own palace content with her own small garden and orchard.

One day Harmony heard that Rhythm had fallen very ill. No one knew if she would live or die. Oh, how Harmony wanted to take some of the tea made from the leaves of her trees to her sister! But she was afraid that Rhythm would think it was a way of saying "I told you so." So she sat there alone in her palace and hoped her sister would recover.

I'm sure you're thinking, just as I did, how silly that was! What did it matter what Rhythm thought of her? The important thing was that Rhythm not die. But all of us do silly things sometimes, especially with the ones we love the most. Sometimes it seems our hearts care so much that our heads don't work right.

But perhaps it was the best decision after all. Or perhaps it was because the trees were flowering and the scent of them got mingled in with Harmony's hopes and the spring breeze blew both the scent and the hopes through the window of a cottage where a little boy lived alone. I never found out if that was what happened but I suspect it was.

The little boy had a young tree growing in his back yard that Queen Harmony gave him when it was a seedling. The boy was too young to know about the Queens' quarrel. It didn't seem strange to him that one Queen lived in the eastern palace and the other Queen lived in the western palace. It had been that way all his life so it seemed normal to him.

The little boy had visited both of the Queens and he loved them both. If he'd ever thought about it at all, he would have thought that the two Queens visited each other.

When the little boy heard about Queen Rhythm's illness, he thought she would take some of the leaves of Queen Harmony's trees, made a tea, drink it, and get well. But then he heard that Queen Rhythm was worse. He was confused. Maybe the royal cooks of the eastern palace didn't know how to prepare the tea correctly.

So one evening - and I think it was the evening that the spring breeze blew - the little boy went out to his own young tree which had only a very few leaves on it. He apologized to the tree for taking the leaves and then went into his kitchen and brewed the tea, hoping that his tree understood and would not lose heart and die.

That night he took the tea in a jar to the eastern palace and gave it to the guard.

"Here is tea for Queen Rhythm," he said. "It's brewed from the leaves of Queen Harmony's trees." And he went home and had a good night's sleep - which I think was very sensible of him. Many older people would have stayed awake worrying about the results.

The next morning Harmony was having her breakfast when a maid announced that a carriage just arrived from the eastern palace.

Rhythm came running in, looking very healthy and happy. "Dear sister! Thank you. Your tea has healed me! How glad I am that you went on that journey after all."

And the sisters hugged and kissed each other and cried all over each other and talked about the years they wasted being apart. And then they hugged and kissed and cried some more until most of us would have been embarrassed and uncomfortable if we'd been there. Not me, of course, I would have liked it.

Then Harmony explained and apologized about not having sent the tea herself. And the sisters began a search, and found the little boy. They adopted him and took him to live with them when they moved back into the Great Castle.

Together they expanded the orchard into many orchards. And their kingdom was happier and healthier and more prosperous than ever. And the air of the kingdom was filled with the fragrance of the blossoms of the trees so that the best poems and most beautiful music in the world came from that kingdom.

When it came time for Queen Harmony and Queen Rhythm to join their parents across the sea, the little boy became King and ruled wonderfully because he had learned much wisdom from both of the sisters.

And all the trees in all the orchards flourished.

But they say that the biggest tree of its kind which produces the loveliest fragrance, the most delicious fruit, and the most powerfully healing leaves, grows in the back yard of an empty cottage where a little boy once lived alone.

Mercy triumphs over judgment.
　　James 2:13

And the leaves of the tree are for the healing of the nations.　Revelation 22:2

Do you think lightly of the riches of His kindness and patience, not knowing the kindness of God leads to repentance?
　　　　　　　　Romans 3:4

The Prince
and his
Well

Once upon a time there was a Prince who lived in a very poor Kingdom. His father the King didn't have enough money to buy him the toys and playthings that most Princes have. When he was still very young, his father said to him, "Son, this kingdom will all be yours some day but right now I have only one thing to give you of your very own."

Then the King led the Prince a short distance from the palace to a grove of trees. In the middle of the trees was a well.

"Here," said the King. "This well is yours."

As you can imagine, the Prince was not very excited about having a well of his own. Not many young Princes would be. Most of them would rather have toy cars and trucks or a ball, or balloons, or even a picture book. But as the Prince grew up, he came to appreciate his well more and more. After running and playing, he was tired and thirsty and he would rest beside the well in the shade of the trees and draw cool water up from its depths in a bucket.

What the Prince did not know was that his well was a very

special well, because he was a very special Prince.

Now you may be thinking it was a wishing well, but it was not. Wishes are very wispy things, see-throughy like smoke or soap bubbles. They're not solid and they don't last long. This is because wishes are usually followed by a 'but'. You know what I mean - "I wish I could go to the ballgame, but I don't have a ride." Or "I wish I had some candy, but I don't have any money." Or "I wish I had a friend to play with, but no one my age lives in this neighborhood."

The Prince often said things like this to the well but since she was not a wishing well, she just sat there sad, and a little confused. For the well was a Willing Well, though the Prince didn't know it.

You never heard of a Willing Well? They are very plentiful and scattered about all over the place but most people, like the Prince, don't know how to use them. The Willing Well worked for the Prince on several occasions but since he didn't know it was a special well, the working seemed to have happened by accident and he didn't know the Well had anything to do with it at all.

One day when the Prince was grown and had just become ruler over his Kingdom, he was resting beside his well. He was very tired from walking over his kingdom trying to meet people and find out all the things that were going on. He said "I wish I had a horse, but I can't afford one." He sat there a few minutes rubbing his aching feet, and his wish turned into a desire.

"I really should have a horse," he said. And he started thinking about how he might acquire one. By the time he sat there an hour, he had several plans in mind. He wasn't sure which plan would work but as he stood up to return to the palace, he patted his well and said, "I WILL have a horse!" And he walked back to the palace feeling pleased with himself.

The Willing Well was pleased too, for she loved to make the Prince happy. Way down deep in the earth, she sent her water traveling far away to the mountain country. Before too long, the water bubbled up into a little spring. Before nightfall, a handsome stallion (one of the wild mountain horses that men try to catch and never can) came by and drank from the spring. His ears perked up! He let out a joyful whinny. Why, this was the most refreshing water he had ever tasted.

The horse started that very moment to follow the scent of the water which he could smell deep under the ground. And he followed it until he came to its source.

The next morning when the Prince went out to his Well, there stood the most beautiful horse he had ever seen. The Prince was overjoyed. And the Well was overjoyed to see the Prince's joy. The horse was overjoyed too because he now had an unending source of the wonderful water, and a new friend as well.

With the horse to ride, the Prince could travel his kingdom much more quickly and his feet were much happier. But the Prince was saddened by what he saw in his kingdom. His people were almost starving.

He sat by his Well one day after a long ride and said, "I wish I could give my people more food and better clothes, and schools and jobs. But I have no money."

As he sat there thinking of the sad faces of the people in his kingdom, his wish turned into a desire. He said "My people really should be able to lead happy, healthy, lives." And he began thinking of several plans for helping his people get their needs met. He didn't know which plan would work but as he stood up to return to the palace, he patted his Well and said, "I WILL help my people!" And he walked back to the palace feeling very pleased with himself.

The Willing Well was very pleased too for now she was

able to do something else for her prince. Way down deep in the earth, she sent her water flowing out, way far away to the sea. The water traveled until it found a fleet of merchant ships bound for a nearby island. Then the water turned into a current which drew the ships like a magnet to the Prince's Kingdom.

When the Prince heard that a fleet of ships had been spotted off shore, he hurried to meet them. The merchants were surprised because they had not known that the Prince's Kingdom even existed.

After several weeks of meeting with the Prince and his people, trading and bartering and agreeing and, we must admit, disagreeing, the merchants sailed away leaving their wares in the kingdom of the Prince, and took with them ships filled with the fruits and minerals of the land of the Kingdom.

By the end of a year, all the people in the Kingdom who wanted jobs had them, making things, refining things, growing things, selling things, teaching things, building things and operating things. The people had plenty to eat and smiles on their faces and rosy cheeks. The children had schools where they learned and played and sang and laughed.

This made the Prince very happy, but all the trading and commerce and education and building meant a lot more work for him and a lot of decisions to make. The Prince began to feel very overburdened with responsibility. And very lonely.

One day he slipped away from his office in the Palace where he spent most of his time now, and went to catch a few minutes of peace beside his well.

He sighed, "I wish I didn't have so much responsibility. But I am the ruler of this Kingdom." As he sat there thinking of the demands on his time and how tired he was, his wish turned into a desire and he said, "I shouldn't have to work so hard." And he began thinking of plans for having more free time. He didn't know which plan would work but as he stood up, he patted his well and said, "I WILL stop having the responsibility of this Kingdom on my shoulders!" And he walked back to the Palace feeling very pleased with himself.

The Willing Well was very pleased too, because she had another opportunity to make her Prince happy. Way down deep in the earth, she sent her water flowing out, far, far away to the sea. The water traveled until it found a warship which belonged to a fierce Prince who wanted to rule a Kingdom but didn't have one. And it began drawing the ship like a magnet.

Oh, dear! This Prince is not at all like our dear Prince, wanting to help people. No, this wicked Prince wanted to rule so that he might have more power than other people and make them work for him instead of themselves. He was most terribly cruel and it would be an awful thing for the people if, after finally beginning a peaceful, fulfilling life in the kingdom for the very first time after all those years of poverty and misery…No! It just won't bear thinking about.

Is there nothing we can do? If the evil, cruel Prince reaches these shores, blood will flow and there will be an end to good times altogether. Quickly! Let's all shout out a warning to our Prince. Perhaps he will hear us and do something before it's too late.

All together now… "Watch out, dear Prince! There is danger ahead!"

Hmmm. I hear some silent spots out there. Come on now. You too!

"Watch out, dear Prince! There is danger ahead!"

That's better!

When the tired Prince went to bed that night, he didn't feel as pleased with himself as he had earlier. He tossed and turned on his bed all night long. The first rays of the sun found him stretched out beside his well.

"I wish I could still help my people and yet have more free

time too, but there is no one to help me govern." As he sat there and thought of his love for his people, his wish turned into a desire and he said, "I should be able to keep on helping my people without having to do it all myself." He began thinking of many plans for changing the government responsibility of his Kingdom. He didn't know which plan would work but as he stood up to return to the Palace, he patted his well and said, "I love my kingdom and won't give it up. But I WILL have others to help me." And he returned to the palace feeling very, very pleased with himself.

The Willing Well was very, very pleased too, for this was the biggest assignment she had ever been given to make her prince happy. Immediately she changed her current into still water, leaving the warship stranded in the sea, not knowing where to go or why it had changed it's course in the first place.

Then way down deep in the earth, the Willing Well sent her waters in many directions, most of them to join rivers and springs right there in the Kingdom, and one of them to a land far across the sea.

Within a few days, people from all over the Kingdom came to the Prince with ideas for a Government Council, and by the end of the month much of the Prince's work was being done by other people who liked it and had been wanting something to do. And nobody was too tired or overworked.

The Prince had more free time to ride his horse and dream beside his well. But he was still lonely. The Willing Well watched his loneliness with patience, and a bit of a smile on her face, for she remembered the current she sent to the land far across the sea.

One day the Prince received a message that a ship with royal sails had been spotted off shore. He hurried to greet the royal ship and when it docked, he was delighted to see the most beautiful Princess in the world walk right down the gangplank and into his Kingdom.

Before that year was over, the Prince and his Princess were happily married. The Prince was very pleased with his responsibilities, very pleased with his Princess, and very pleased with his Kingdom.

And the Willing Well was very, very, very pleased because her Prince was happy.

And we will all be very, very, very pleased if the cruel prince and his warship remain puzzled and stranded in the middle of the sea until the end of time.

Won't we?

...select capable men from all the people - men who fear God, trustworthy men who hate dishonest gain - and appoint them as officials...That will make your load lighter, because they will share it with you...and they will go home satisfied.
Exodus 18: 21-23

If any of you lack wisdom, let him ask of God, that gives to all me liberally, and does not upbraid, and it shall be given him. But let him ask in faith, nothing wavering. For he that wavers is like a wave of the sea driven with the wind and tossed. For let not that man think that he shall receive anything of the Lord. A double minded man is unstable in all his ways.
James 1:5-8

It is not good for man to be alone.
Genesis 2:18

Princess Jeanetta
and the War

Once upon a time, there was a little princess named Jeanetta. She was much loved by her parents, the King and Queen. They took very good care of their daughter, for even before her birth they received serious orders from the High King concerning her care.

Jeanetta was a very special princess and the High King had important plans for her future, although no one knew them but the High King Himself.

Princess Jeanetta lived in a kingdom called Whitania. If you looked on a map, you would see that it is parallel with the kingdom of Blackovia. You would see this and I can see it, but strangely enough no one in either of the two kingdoms had ever noticed. They shared the same climate, the same economic endeavors, the same recreational fun, and yet the two tiny kingdoms had been at war for centuries.

Indeed, little Princess Jeanetta was born into a world where every kingdom was at war with every other kingdom. She never understood this, even from the time she was a tiny princess, for unknown to her parents or anyone else, she had arrived in Whitania with a special commission of her own from the High King - to declare an end to war. Princess Jeanetta was especially anxious to see her nation become friendly with Blackovia since it lay closest to them in location.

Little Princess Jeanetta began early at her mission of peace, crossing the border to play or share her possessions with the Blackovian citizens who lived near the border. Some of these citizens could see the beauty and sincerity of the princess and became her friends. Others just took the gifts she offered and despised her for giving them. Still others hated all Whitanians so much that they wouldn't let her near them.

The King and Queen did not know what to do about this strange behavior of their daughter. They knew, in theory, that all the kingdoms were equal under the High King. But they didn't understand about Jeanetta's special commission so they were afraid for her and discouraged those very activities for which the High King had sent her.

Princess Jeanetta grew in grace and beauty, and she learned many things and she did many good works. But always there was a longing to do the very thing no one seemed to want her to do - bring about peace between the two kingdoms.

While the princess was growing and learning in Whitania, there was something special going on in Blackovia.

Prince Wilhelm had been sent by the High King into Blackovia with - yes, you guessed it - the very same commission as our princess. Prince Willie, as he was called by those who loved him, was greatly favored in his kingdom. He was kind and generous and became a champion of the oppressed among his people. He was sent as their representative to many gatherings of the Council of Kingdoms.

The High King was pleased with these two who would fulfill His plan for peace among the kingdoms. One day He sent a message to each of them to come to Him in the woods at the border of their two lands.

At first Prince Willie and Princess Jeanetta were shy with each other because they had both been taught that there could be no real understanding or friendship between their people. But as the day went on they discovered that they were more alike than either of them were with the people of their own kingdoms.

It was a wonderful, glorious day for both of them. And when evening came, they parted with many plans and promises for days to come.

But alas! As in all real tales of adventure, there was an Enemy! The Wicked Grundge lived in the Icy Region of the Land of Fearinski. It wasn't really a kingdom at all, but the Wicked Grundge had convinced everyone that it was, and that he was a real king, and should be given influence in Council Affairs.

Indeed, it was this same Wicked Grundge who was behind all the wars, though nobody knew it and believed they had thought up the wars themselves. The Grundge had infiltrated all the kingdoms by sending his dastardly Evil Gorches to spy and stir up trouble at every opportunity.

On the day when Prince Willie and Princess Jeanetta met in the woods at the border, Gorch spies from both kingdoms hurried to report to the Grundge.

The Wicked Grundge clasped his evil hands together and began wringing them in tormented despair. "No! This must not be! It would put an end to my Lifework! If those two who are closest to the thrones should become allies, why think of the destruction to my hold on the kingdoms! He shuddered, as if the thought was too horrible to contemplate, and then went on. "It would be just the start. The…" Here he stopped again, as if the words did not want to pass through his vocal chords, "the acceptance…and, and…trust, and…love, Yech!...would begin there and spread thoughout Blacovia and Whitania. Horrid thought! And then…" He tugged at the icy strands atop his evil head. "It wouldn't stop there. The other kingdoms will catch it. Indavia, Asiandia!"

The Grundge's voice had ascended almost to a scream and the shrill pitch was rattling icicles in the cave ceiling above him. "And then there would be…No, I can't say it." The Grundge gagged, and lowered his voice to a tremulous whisper. "There would be…" He spat out the words. "Peace…and Brotherhood…among mankind."

The Grundge lowered himself into a chair, all of his energies depleted by the horrifying thought.

The Gorches stood silently throughout this rampage, trying to still the knocking of their skinny knees. If this news had so shaken their Terrible Leader, what would be their reward for being its messengers?

The Wicked Grundge sat staring at the floor of the icy cavern for a long, awful space of time. When he lifted his head, there was a malevolent gleam in his eyes which the Gorches recognized. It did nothing to still the tremor in their limbs.

"You will stop it!" He looked at each of them in turn with a terrible smile. His voice was deadly calm. "Yes, my trusty servants, you will stop this calamity from happening. You will put an end to this madness before it goes further. Yes, you will. Yes! You will!"

"But…but…How, Your Awfulness? How?"

The stillness was broken as the Grundge's voice soared again to a shriek. "I care not how. Just do it!" As if to give emphasis to the command, a giant icicle fell from above them, stabbing through the snow at their feet, and stood quivering not three inches from the nose of the middle one of them.

Without another word, the Gorches withdrew.

Now you mustn't think that they got together to plan a

strategy such as you and I would have done. No, Gorches have no concept of working together. They left, each with its own idea of how to carry out its assignment.

Gorches are not very smart. They have no originality or creativity. But we must say this for them - they are persistent. They do not give up. One cannot, of course, couple the word virtue with the word Gorch in any area, but if one could, that virtue would be tenacity.

Oh my! What our dear Prince and Princess went through was unbearable. Night and day they were tormented by the Gorches. I would not cause you to share their misery by relating the exact details of the torture, but on and on it went until our hero and heroine were quite beside themselves with weariness and pain.

Our beautiful Princess Jeanetta ended up in a sickbed in an isolated tower room of her palace, and our courageous Prince Willie could be seen wandering in the dark dungeons of his own castle, unable to find a way out. The bruises each of them received made movement slow and difficult, and the agonies of pain made them not only reluctant to move, but it confused their minds so that it seemed there could never be any future beyond sickbed and dungeon.

Our hearts shudder and our eyes shed a tear or two as we turn from this dreadful scene.

Do I…?

Yes. I do. I hear you asking the very same question that I asked.

"WHY WERE THE GORCHES ALLOWED TO PERPETRATE SUCH WICKEDNESS ON OUR PRINCE AND PRINCESS?"

I asked it. Right out loud. And no one answered my question. And if you have asked it, I daresay that no one has answered yours either. They stare, or avoid your eyes, or change the subject, or they shrug and say "It can't be helped." But give you an explanation, they don't!

It seemed that this miserable state of affairs would continue indefinitely. But one day, when the princess had a teeny bit of strength, she wrote a letter. It's not important to know to whom she wrote it. And quite frankly, I tried to find out. But the opinion seemed to be that if we discovered who it was that answered her letter, we would all bombard that one person with letters and they wouldn't be able to get on with their real duties for answering our letters. The important thing was the Response Itself.

It was a very simple response. It merely reminded the Princess about the High King's RULEBOOK FOR KINGDOMS.

Princess Jeanetta had a copy brought to her immediately, and as soon as she read the recommended part, she leaped out of her bed and ordered her carriage.

Before much time had passed she crossed the border and entered the courtyard of the Castle of Blackovia. She demanded that the startled guards tell her the whereabouts of the prince. One of the guards was a Gorch in disguise who tried to stop her, but it was too late. She had discovered in the Rulebook that Gorches had no legal right in the kingdoms. She reminded it that if it gave trouble, it would be sent back to the Grundge immediately. After its last experience in the Icy Regions, it was easily convinced to withdraw further objections.

The princess quickly made her way to the dungeon door. She could barely see her dear Willie there in the gloom, through the bars on the door.

"Willie! Over here! The way out is here," she called.

The prince, looking very battered and unprincelike, stumbled to the door. "You? Here?"

"Yes, it's me. Now come out!"

He squinted his eyes as if he could hardly see her, although she was standing in the light. Perhaps he had been in the dark so long that the light blinded him. "How do I know it's really you?"

"Don't be silly, Willie," said the princess. "You know my voice. Of course it's me."

"Are you going to hurt me?" asked the prince in a rather quivery sort of voice.

"Of course not," she laughed. "Now come on out."

"I can't," he said. "The door's locked."

"But look!" She pointed. "The key is right there on your side. Just unlock the door and come on out."

He paused. "How do I know you aren't tricking me?"

At this point our princess did a very unprincesslike thing. But if you knew that she had been quite as weak and ill as the prince, and that it was only her love and trust in him that gave her the strength to write that letter that was the beginning of her own convalescence…well, if you knew that, perhaps you could understand and forgive her.

She…I do hate to tell you, but that's the way real stories are. There are always bits and pieces you would rather leave out in the telling. She stomped her feet at the prince. She stuck out her tongue at the prince. And she said…(can you bear to hear it?) "You are stupid! Just like the rest of your stupid kingdom!"

And she whirled around and left him standing there holding onto the bars of the door to his prison. Princess Jeanetta leaped into her carriage and drove to the woods at the border where she first met the prince. She threw herself onto the grass and began beating the ground with her fists and screaming.

After a time of this sort of carrying on, she was too exhausted to continue it any longer. And I still say that the whole thing was due to her still being weak from her own illness.

But be that as it may, when her temper tantrum was over

and she stopped screaming enough to hear, and stopped crying enough to see, she realized that the High King was standing there talking to her.

In a short while, she was in her carriage with a smile on her face heading back to the dungeon where Prince Willie was captive. He stood just as she had left him.

"Dear Prince," she said gently. "I'm sorry for how I acted and what I said. I didn't mean it. Look Here is the High King's RULEBOOK FOR KINGDOMS." She held it up for him to see through the bars. "Look! The Wicked Grundge and those Gorches are the cause of all our problems. And they never had any right in our kingdoms. We could have kicked them out years ago. And to think we let them make us sick and imprison us! We've all been silly. But please, come out now."

The prince looked hopeful and sad all at the same time. "I'd like to, Jeanetta. Really I would. But I'm not sure. If only I could just be sure!"

Remembering what the High King told her, the princess smiled. "I understand. Here." She passed the Rulebook through the bars. "You take this and if you'll stay near the door where there is light to see, why then you can read it. And you'll be sure."

The prince took the book but he didn't say anything.

"I must go now," the princess said softly.

Fear sprang into the prince's eyes. "No! Don't leave me!"

"I really must," she replied. "I'll be waiting for you at the border, in our woods.

Princess Jeanetta spent a peaceful afternoon in the woods with the High King. They sang together and walked along the brook together. He explained to her more about her commission in the kingdoms. Then they sat quietly side by side under a large tree for a while. Suddenly the princess heard the pounding of horses' hooves. She looked up and...

You guessed it! It was the prince. He was free, and dressed in finery, looking more noble and courageous than ever. He leaped from the horse and knelt at the feet of the High King.

The King raised him up and put the princesses hand in his. "Now go," said the High King.

And they did!

Back in the Icy Regions, the Grundge was getting very nervous. He received no word from his Gorches for a long time. Then, one at a time, they began slinking back into the ice caverns, first from the kingdoms of Blackovia and Whitania, and then from the neighboring kingdoms, and then from all over the earth.

They were a pitiful sight, if one could possibly pity a Gorch. Mere shadows of their former selves, weakened beyond recognition, they crawled in, slithered in, dragged themselves in, Gorch by Gorch.

A few of them gasped, "Too warm out there." But that's all the information the Wicked Grundge could get.

No matter how hard he kicked them.

And we have known and believed the love that God has to us. God is love; and the one who dwells in love dwells in God, and God in him. This is the way our love is made perfect, so that we may have boldness in the day of judgment; because as He is, so are we in this world. There is no fear in love; but perfect love casts out fear because fear has torment. He that fears is not made perfect in love.
I John 4:16-18

Jesus said to them "It is the spirit that makes alive; the flesh doesn't profit anything. The words I speak to you, they are spirit and they are life." John 6:63

Sanctify them through Your truth. Your Word is truth. John 17:17.

Jesus… gave them authority over unclean spirits.
Mark 6:7

God has not given us a spirit of fear but of power, love, and a sound mind.
II Timothy 1:7

www.ingramcontent.com/pod-product-compliance
Lightning Source LLC
Chambersburg PA
CBHW051245170626
46809CB00004B/1496